T0282870

ALLEGIANCE

ESSENTIAL PROSE SERIES 212

Guernica Editions Inc. acknowledges the support of
the Canada Council for the Arts and the Ontario Arts Council.
The Ontario Arts Council is an agency of the Government of Ontario.

We acknowledge the financial support of the Government of Canada.

MICHAEL SPRINGATE

ALLEGIANCE

GUERNICA
EDITIONS

TORONTO • CHICAGO • BUFFALO • LANCASTER (U.K.)
2023

Guernica Founder: Antonio D'Alfonso

Michael Mirolla, editor
Interior and cover design: Rafael Chimicatti
Guernica Editions Inc.
287 Templemead Drive, Hamilton, ON L8W 2W4
2250 Military Road, Tonawanda, N.Y. 14150-6000 U.S.A.
www.guernicaeditions.com

Distributors:
Independent Publishers Group (IPG)
600 North Pulaski Road, Chicago IL 60624
University of Toronto Press Distribution (UTP)
5201 Dufferin Street, Toronto (ON), Canada M3H 5T8

First edition.
Printed in Canada.

Legal Deposit—Third Quarter
Library of Congress Catalog Card Number: 2023930015
Library and Archives Canada Cataloguing in Publication
Title: Allegiance / Michael Springate.
Names: Springate, Michael, 1952- author.
Series: Essential prose series ; 212.
Description: Series statement: Essential prose series ; 212
Identifiers: Canadiana (print) 2023013498X
Canadiana (ebook) 20230135013 | ISBN 9781771838429 (softcover)
ISBN 9781771838436 (EPUB)
Classification: LCC PS8587.P74 A75 2023 | DDC C813/.54—dc23

*"Now is the time to understand more,
so that we may fear less."*
—Marie Curie

THE FIRST GATE
Alexandria
2009

CHAPTER ONE

"A RE YOU FROM ENGLAND? I mean, your accent … "
"Luo is my first language. My parents are from Kenya, but I studied at the University of Sussex and worked hard to achieve it. Do you think the BBC would accept me? Not that I'd ever work for them, you understand, I have some self-respect." She laughed, a vigorous woman in her early forties clearing a heavy stack of files from a small round table. "This is where my volunteer usually works. By the window. She's not here today. Actually, she's rarely here. I need a new volunteer." She gestured, inviting him to sit. "Do you like Alexandria?"

"Too soon to say. I arrived this morning."

"Is it your first time here?"

"My first trip out of North America."

"Not even to Europe?"

"I had a stopover in Frankfurt on my way to Cairo, does that count?"

She laughed. "We're even. I've never been to America and I haven't a clue what it's like. Mind you, I have my opinions."

"Your first name, is it actually Perpetua?"

"Yes."

"Are you named after the martyr?"

"Very few people ask that. At least they didn't in England. You surprise me." She crossed back to her desk, its surface covered by various heights of stacked folders, grasped an electric kettle and plugged it in, then returned to sit with him.

"She died in the arena," he said. "A martyr."

"Yes, in Carthage. Tunis today."

They both understood he wasn't there for that conversation. Victor placed a large envelope on the table. "The lawyer in Cairo wanted me to meet you. He thinks you will be able to help locate a young man from Montreal, Mahfouz, my daughter's partner. I have the basic information for you: his full name, date of birth in Cairo, date of Canadian naturalization. He left a coloured photocopy of the first page of his passport with his parents so I brought a copy of that. I have two other photos. The first was taken on the day of his graduation from university about a year ago, and the other is from earlier this summer. The girl laughing beside him is my daughter, Elena. The little girl in front is Sharon, my grandchild."

Perpetua withdrew the materials and slowly read the information. Then she looked at the photocopy of the passport. Lastly, she held each of the photos and looked at them with equal intent. "The girl, did you say her name was Sharon? She looks so happy. It's quite a wonderful picture, the three of them."

"Mahfouz and Elena only met this year. Sharon is the child of a previous relationship."

"Ah." Perpetua nodded and looked away, formulating a question, then returned to the pictures without asking it. She rose to finish preparing the tea. Serving the cups she asked, "And why does your lawyer think I can help find him?"

"He said you have contacts in the prisons that others don't. We believe he is being held by the police, and want to know for certain if that's the case."

"Did you ask the authorities if they're holding him?"

"They insist they aren't."

"You don't believe them?"

"They lie, don't they?"

"Not all the time," she answered drily. "Did you coordinate your request with the Canadian government? It's they who should be asking. It would make a difference if they asked."

"Our government acknowledges he's missing, but doesn't take that fact too seriously."

"That wasn't my question. Did they ask the Egyptian government?"

"They say they did, and received the same reply."

Perpetua hesitated. "You don't want to hear this, but what you're asking is beyond my abilities."

"You won't help?" Victor asked, surprised.

"I've had success locating people in an incoherent system, but I've never succeeded in locating someone the government wants hidden. That's what you're suggesting, isn't it?"

"You won't try?"

She answered by slipping the printed pages and photographs into the envelope and giving it back.

"I was hoping to leave that with you," he said.

"I'm not opening a file."

"Alexandria is a long way to come for a cup of tea."

"I'm sorry."

"He said this was the right way forward … the lawyer. He insisted I meet you, give you this information, put up a poster."

"He should have saved you the trip."

"But he didn't." Victor took a sip of the tea. "Can I offer your organization a donation?"

Perpetua rooted the palms of her hands flat on the table. "It doesn't work like that. We always need funds but I haven't asked for any and won't change my mind if you give any."

"I'm not trying to insult you. I'm trying to understand."

"The prison system here is very large; the cases on my desk more than I can handle. I won't abandon those I can help to open files on those I can't."

"I'm not going to change your mind, am I?" he asked.

"Not with the information you've offered. Even if I put aside my doubts whether I can help, the majority of those I serve don't have legal representation. You can afford a lawyer. Duplicating efforts is a misuse of my time."

"Can I tape a poster on your wall?"

"I'm sorry …"

"I've made copies of Mahfouz's graduation photo. The lawyer told me to put one here. He was explicit. His phone number in Cairo is on the front, my own contact information – should you ever need it – is on the back. What harm can it do to take one? Seriously … what harm?"

"You're persistent. All right, put him there." She pointed to an empty space beside an ageing photo of a smiling young couple. "Beside my parents."

Victor affixed the poster beside the photo using snippets of two-sided tape. He wanted to begin the conversation over, to find a different way to gain her support, but when he turned she was waiting for him at the door. He crossed towards her. "I appreciate you taking the time to meet me," he said, grasping her outstretched hand.

"I'm sorry I can't help," Perpetua replied, letting him go.

She shut the door behind him and refreshed her tea. The leaves were stale, that was the problem. She looked out the window, wondering how her son was doing. She hoped he would visit soon. She turned to look at the picture of her parents. She liked that photo, the evident affection between them. She considered Mahfouz's captured gaze and decided he was shy and naturally reserved. Well, she'd leave the poster up for a bit; it could do no harm even if it did no good. She had no difficulty believing he had been held by the security forces – for whatever reason – but she thought it unlikely he was still suffering. When the Egyptian government denied any trace of someone it was often to avoid being questioned over an unexplained death.

She went to her desk and began to work, the foreign traveller's concerns no longer in mind.

* * *

Victor returned to the economy hotel on the top floor of an ageing building that had seen better days. The elevator being broken, he climbed the stairs spiralling around the elevator shaft. The first two floors had a variety of well-appointed offices with various professional titles on the wide doors. The succeeding floors offered more modest hallways with narrow doors, many of which, or so it occurred to him, were rarely opened. He arrived at the fifth floor breathing heavily. He barely acknowledged the polite nod of the receptionist. He used the old-fashioned metal key to open the door to his room. Although it was still mid-afternoon he immediately lay on his side, curled in self-defence, and fell asleep.

He awoke in pitch dark, took off his shoes, his clothes, then slipped between the sheets, finally stretching out.

He awoke well before dawn. He did not feel refreshed, but not tired either. Unsure what to do he turned on the light, went to the tiny sink to brush his teeth and wash his face.

He put on his clothes and pocketed the two-sided tape. He picked up one of his posters for the missing Mahfouz and followed the corridor back to the reception area.

The young man who greeted him earlier was still there, feet on the desk, softly tapping out a rhythm on the arm of his chair. In the small alcove opposite the desk, a person Victor had not previously seen lay splayed on an upholstered couch, muttering softly in his dreams.

"I don't mean to bother you …" Victor said quietly, addressing the receptionist who immediately swung his legs to the ground and removed the headphones.

"Can I help?"

"I have a picture of a missing person. I would like to put it up."

"I don't understand."

"May I put up a poster of a missing person?"

"Here? You want to put it here?"

"If you don't mind."

"But why? Who is going to see it here?"

"I understand it seems unlikely, but if by some chance a visitor or someone who works here recognizes him, they can phone the number on the front. A poster hanging here won't do any harm, will it? Would you mind?"

"Let me take a look." The receptionist considered the image and then nodded approval. "He's young, your friend. There's space over there."

Victor turned and, among advertisements for bus tours and tourist destinations, saw an empty space on the wall above the sleeping figure. He began by preparing the small pieces of tape.

"I can't promise it will stay up long," the receptionist said.

Victor leaned over the figure and flattened the picture carefully against the wall. He stepped back, pleased with his small victory. He started towards the stairs and then stopped. "Is there anything open at this hour? Some place to eat?"

"Not now. It's much too early. Later."

"Well, I'd like some fresh air. It's safe, isn't it, to go out?"

The young man stood. "I'll come with you."

"You don't have to."

"I want to smoke and the owners prefer I do that outside. No one is going to miss me for a few minutes and besides, Yasser is here." The sleeping figure, hearing his name, managed to rearrange his legs.

They descended the flights and exited onto a narrow street. The younger man opened a new pack of cigarettes and offered one. "My name is Hakim."

Victor waved the cigarette away. "Victor."

"Yes. I registered you."

"Do you always work both day and night?"

"I'd rather work two shifts back-to-back than have two jobs. Yasser has two jobs. He works as a cleaner at night and in a kitchen across the city during the day. He doesn't have time to go home in between so I let him sleep on our couch."

"There isn't an empty room?"

"I couldn't do that."

"I'm sorry if I disturbed him."

Hakim shrugged his shoulders.

An emaciated orange and white cat with swollen dugs stepped out of the darkness. She slipped sideways and, keeping low, stopped at the edge of a small puddle formed by a dripping air conditioner two floors up. She appeared to study the men before cautiously lowering her head to lap. Two white kittens appeared as rays of light from the gloom behind, stumbling over each other, playful. They, too, began to drink. Hakim and Victor watched silently.

"Beautiful, aren't they?" Hakim asked.

"The sea is close, isn't it?"

"At the end of the street."

"I'd like to see it."

They followed the street to its end and stepped away from the buildings. The dark water undulated before them. The wind – soft – rolled over its expanse. The sky – immense – soared above containing a myriad of stars.

Hakim gestured towards the sea. "This whole area has been mapped using all sorts of equipment: aerial photography, sonar readings, core sampling, magnetometers. They did the same with the Bay of Abū Qīr … that way." He looked to his right. "They were looking for Napoleon's ship, *The Orient*, but found something more important."

"What could be more important than Napoleon's ship?" Victor asked, enjoying his own humour.

"Ancient cities. They were looking for two that had disappeared. They had written evidence for each, yet nothing of either had been found. Eventually they detected ruins covered by a thick layer of sediment. Beneath the ruins were ancient artifacts. Studying those it became clear they had discovered one city with two names – Thonis for the Egyptians and Heracleion among the Greeks."

Victor's thoughts had drifted. He wanted to know about the sour smell, which irked him. Was it gas? But from where? He also wanted to know why he couldn't hear birds. At this time of the morning he expected to hear birds.

Hakim continued. "The city must have sunk as the ground settled during earthquakes. Then the Nile did its thing, depositing sediment. They say the rising sea is going to swallow most of this coast, including where we're standing."

"Really? Here?"

"An effect of global warming."

"What's being done about it?"

Hakim laughed. "Something should be done? Other than talking?"

"I mean," Victor said, "if it's going to be a problem."

"It's already a problem. At least to the farmers. The rising water table leeches salt into the soil, destroying crops at the root. Nothing can grow on once fertile fields."

They retraced their steps and entered the old building at ground level. Victor hesitated, daunted by the stairs, but chose not to mention the broken elevator. When they arrived at the top Hakim re-established himself behind the desk. Victor checked the poster. It was still there, clearly visible. The man on the couch had disappeared.

"It's like that six days of seven," Hakim said. "I wake Yasser and go out for a smoke while he uses the washroom to wash and change. If I take too long he simply leaves. It's not a problem, no one ever calls or visits at this hour. Will you go to the new Library? You can walk to it from here. They have a sculpture out front that was pulled from the bay. It was underwater for at least a thousand years."

"I'm not really here for the tourist thing."

"I understand, but if you do find the time, what I like best – what I recommend – are the catacombs of Kom el Shoqafa. Often visitors don't get there, but they should."

"What do you like about it?"

"The feeling. If you sit there a while, underground …"

"I don't understand."

"That's why you should go."

* * *

He had again fallen asleep fully clothed, but this time awoke with the room bathed in light. He was aware of having woken earlier, of talking to the receptionist, going outside and seeing the bay, but his memories of it were already vague. He heard the fragments of a conversation in the corridor.

A man's voice. "Pretend ... explain ... won't happen." Then a woman with a strong accent. "People ... no point, but ..." Then a voice he recognized. "... always more bullets than people ..."

Laughter.

Victor liked the laughter. He wanted to join in. He rose and quietly opened the door. Hakim turned to face him. "I'm sorry if we're bothering you."

"You're not bothering me." Victor opened the door wider. "I appreciate hearing laughter."

"We're talking about the riots in Greece," the other man said.

"Are there riots in Greece?" Victor asked, turning towards him.

Hakim intervened. Nodding towards Victor he said, "Victor arrived from Canada yesterday." Turning to the couple he added, "Oksanna and Nikos are also guests at the hotel."

"I've been to Canada," the woman with the tight braids said.

"Ah?" Victor prompted.

"I was confused." She stopped abruptly, creating an awkward silence. "I mean," she said, starting again, "it's a very big country."

Victor wanted to hear more. He gestured into his untidy room. "There's a hotplate in my room and I can offer tea."

The woman laughed in surprise. It was a beautiful, cascading, and spontaneous laugh.

Victor smiled. "I don't have four cups, but ..." He placed his palms against his temples then ran his hands through his hair to the back of his skull where his fingers entangled, and remained. He decided to make a direct appeal to the young couple. "I know what I'm about to say is unusual, but I've never been in a situation like this before and I don't know how to move forward. I'm hoping you can help me."

"Victor is looking for a missing person," Hakim said.

"Missing since the summer," Victor said.

Hakim touched Victor's elbow, reminding him he could lower his arms, which he did. "This isn't the best place for a conversation," Hakim said. "Maybe we should all meet again later."

"I'm not sure why we'd get involved," the man said. "We're not from here. One should go to the police, no?"

"We've met with the authorities," Victor replied. "But maybe that's not enough. Maybe there's a better way to approach the problem. All I'm asking for is a conversation. You can forget about me afterwards."

"There's nothing wrong with a conversation," the woman said.

The man shrugged, giving way.

"Let's all meet at my desk at eight," Hakim said. "We can go somewhere for a bite."

"I'd like that. At eight. Thank you." Victor looked at each in turn, hoping to personalize Hakim's decision. "Thank you. Thank you." He backed into his room and closed the door.

His open notebook lay upside down beside the cell phone on the small desk. There was a second pair of pants hanging neatly over the back of the chair with a spare shirt over it. He looked at the light blue bedspread fallen on the floor. It matched the painted abstract on the wall. He noted he was holding his breath, as if trying to join the stillness and fuse with the surroundings. He exhaled. He needn't be so anxious. Nervous and disoriented, perhaps, but he had started. Hakim agreed to a meeting as if it was the most natural thing in the world. The circle was widening, which was the point.

Eventually the right information would get to the right person. Perpetua had rejected him but he could deal with that.

He needed to walk through the city and put up more posters.

CHAPTER TWO

ON MONDAY EVENING at five past eight, Oksanna, Nikos, and Victor stood awkwardly in front of the reception desk.

"Why don't you take Victor and see if you can get a table," Hakim said to Oksanna. "Nikos and I will follow when my replacement comes."

"Are you sure?" Oksanna replied.

"There's no reason for us all to hang around."

Victor knew the elevator hadn't been repaired but pushed the service button anyhow. A squawking started somewhere high above, the steel cables tightened, a motor groaned, the cables further tightened … nothing moved.

"We're meeting for a sad reason," Oksanna said as they took the stairs. "It's different when people meet for sad reasons. They have to be less funny, more honest."

"Are you Greek?" Victor asked.

"Why Greek?"

"You were discussing the riots there."

"I'm from Ukraine. Born in Slavyansk but studied and worked in Odessa, where Nikos and I met. Now I live in Athens."

"You've been together a while?"

"Half a year. For me it's a small miracle. He calls it his bad luck."

"He's not serious. Is he?"

Again the wonderful sound of cascading laughter. "He had an interview at the University for the position of lecturer. He wanted the job very much but ended up in a shouting match with the committee interviewing him. That night, to drown his sorrows, he found a bar and a woman. She was living with me at the time. When she brought him home he and I started a conversation. At some point he decided it was more interesting arguing with me than having sex with her. He told me he'd stay in touch, and he did."

Oksanna chose a table as far as possible from either of the two large screens, both filled with the same face of a thin man talking to a bored host. The waiter appeared with a pair of menus. Oksanna indicated they would be four. The waiter returned with two more menus and four small bottles of cold water.

"What do you do in Canada?" she asked.

"I'm a mechanic. I work on cars."

"Could you get work here?"

"I could get the job done, assuming tools and parts."

"It must be nice to have skills you can take anywhere. I'm an actor. I can't find work in Athens because of my accent."

"I'd never have guessed you were an actor."

She gave him a quick smile. "That's good! People don't usually respect actors. Especially if they are blond and female. At least not in Greece. They think the worst."

He laughed. "Yes, I can imagine."

"Can you?" she asked, as if wounded.

"I take that back. I was trying to agree with you. I wasn't trying to imagine anything."

She paused. "But now you are?"

"No! Not at all!"

"Nikos says I'm my own worst enemy. I'm too direct. But direct is good, isn't it?"

The two men arrived. "Lamia," Nikos said, as if announcing something important.

"How do you know?" Hakim asked.

"Trust me. We're at fifteen. How about Rhodes?"

"I think so. Okay, sixteen."

Nikos sat beside Victor. "Between us we can name sixteen Greek cities which had demonstrations. The media began by claiming it was all because of a student's death in Athens. They said it went national because of the anarchists. Did you know we had that many anarchists waiting for a student to die so they could riot?"

Hakim made himself comfortable. "They want an excuse. They don't want to report that good people are on the street doing things they've never done before, terrified of being arrested."

"If you burn down a building …" Oksanna interjected.

"You're an arsonist," Nikos replied. "Not an anarchist. Hakim is right. It's what they want us to believe."

"Victor is a car mechanic," Oksanna said. "He can find a job anywhere."

"Is that what you do?" Hakim asked.

Victor nodded.

"See that! A useful man! Useful!" Nikos exclaimed. "I'm an honest economist. Look at me and weep!"

"I would think that's the best kind," Victor said, trying to see beyond the self-mockery.

"Oksanna is a brilliant actress," Nikos said. "Brilliant. I've seen her perform many times. But now she lives in the wrong city with a man who can't support her. Hakim? He's an archeologist wasting his talents as a receptionist in a crappy hotel in a good location."

"Is that true?" Victor asked, turning to Hakim.

"That it's a crappy hotel in a good location?"

"Being an archeologist?"

"No."

"He's modest," Nikos said. "He studies people by what they leave behind, not by what they say. He'd rather sift through your trash than listen to you speak. Isn't that an archeologist?"

A large party arrived, an extended family with invited guests. They milled at the door, not quite sure if they should enter. The staff suddenly appeared armed with dozens of pink balloons which they placed on the empty tables. The children immediately raced forward to play with them, batting them high in the air with their hands, kicking them along the floor. The adults moved in behind their advance guard and now confidently claimed the space. The sound of electronic disco music, volume cranked up, suddenly assaulted the room, leaving the conversation on the two screens a dumb show.

"We're not going to be able to talk!" Oksanna yelled at Nikos.

"What did you say?" he shouted.

"We're supposed to talk. About the missing person!"

Nikos clearly didn't understand what she had said. "I'm sorry?" he yelled, but just as he did so the music stopped and his words, asked as a question, rang out in the restaurant. The party turned to see who was making so much noise.

As suddenly as it disappeared the music began again, this time as a happy love song driven by a sampled beat.

"Slightly better," Hakim yelled, twisting in his seat to witness the event unfold.

Victor felt lost. He had worried about what to say but now wondered if he would be able to say anything. Oksanna read his thoughts. She put her hand on his forearm and leaned towards his ear. "Expect nothing and it will all work out." She leaned back and looked straight at him, giving him a moment to catch up. He raised his arms, not too high, in mock surrender. She smiled, nodded.

The beleaguered waiter appeared to take their order.

Yet more guests arrived. The women, expensively dressed, very few in head coverings, with men wearing suits. The staff quickly conferred in a huddle, broke apart. The children continued running from table to table, yelling at cousins, aunts and uncles, trying to capture the balloons which occasionally burst. Into this happy chaos arrived a well-dressed couple. Two portable spotlights, joined on a short bar and raised high on a long pole, suddenly burst into light. The women stood as one, turned towards the young couple and ululated. The men, too, stood and applauded. More balloons burst. A man holding a camera began to record the event. He first focused on the couple, then slowly panned around the room, coordinating his movements with the spotlights. One by one the women were framed by the light, each renewing her rejoicing.

Victor identified the father of the bride-to-be, grey haired in a grey suit, a successful patriarch. He felt happy for the man as he enjoyed what must be a very special evening. The music continued, breathless and overwhelming.

The food finally arrived at the table in the corner. They ate in imposed silence, spectators to the evening. As soon as he finished Hakim gestured for the bill, waving off the efforts of the others to share in its payment. Outside, he grabbed Oksanna's arm and insisted they walk together. Nikos and Victor followed in their wake.

Hakim led them on the main road, then turned into a dense warren of narrow streets filled with brightly lit shops.

The entire area went dark.

"It happens all the time," Hakim explained, not slowing, as he led them deeper into the maze. "Water stops running, electricity is turned off. They won't notice at The Imperial. That part of the city is never affected."

Sharp instructions overlapped from different directions as generators were rolled onto the sidewalks. The rapid hacking of gas-fed engines filled the night. Shopkeepers without electricity placed lit candles throughout their stores and sat at the entrances. Business continued.

"Tourists come to Egypt to see the past," Nikos said to Victor. "It would make more sense if they came to see the future. Individuals can apply their separate bandages, like the generators or candles, but it doesn't solve the problem."

"Is this the future we should expect?"

"Give it time. When there's no investment in infrastructure a place falls apart. London will be like Cairo, New York like Alexandria."

"That has to be an exaggeration."

"Do you think the cities of Egypt didn't have their glory days? Seeing the Anglo-American empire against a longer time scale might surprise you, but it shouldn't."

The hammerings of the generators faded into a tolerable thrum as they walked deeper into the darkness. Victor felt relieved when they settled into a candle-lit tea shop, joining a dozen silhouettes and shadows speaking in calm voices, smoking shisha, speaking on cell phones.

"Do you want to play backgammon?" Hakim asked Oksanna.

Victor watched as she set off to find a board and pieces. Soon their hands, fluent and swift, threw dice and moved markers, clicking each into its momentary place, showing no hesitation. Victor understood that strategic decisions were woven into their pace, but it was all too quick for him to decipher.

Oksanna won the first game and immediately started a second.

Nikos thumbed through messages on his phone. Victor wanted to pursue the earlier conversation. "Anglo-American empire. That's what you said. I've never heard that term before."

"Have you been living under a rock?"

Victor was stung. "I've heard British Empire and American Empire, of course, but not an Anglo-American Empire."

Nikos looked up. "But you understand. It makes sense to you. Same enterprise, same intentions, now joined."

"Who is in this empire? Is Europe a part of it?"

"Yes," Hakim answered, obviously overhearing their conversation.

Nikos snorted. "We argue about it. For now he's right."

"Nikos doesn't want the alliance to last," Hakim said before blowing on the dice.

"I don't think it should last," Nikos said.

"Why not?" Victor asked.

"Because the priority of the Anglo-American empire is to ensure that the wealthy get wealthier. To them that's the first and only principle of good government."

Victor hesitated before speaking. "I don't know if that's true. When there's too much inequality there is debate, discussion. New policies emerge."

Nikos was surprised by what he took to be Victor's naïveté. "In all empires there are periods of wealth consolidation followed by stagnation and decline. It's not so easy to fight, let alone reverse."

Oksanna won the second game. She asked if they were playing best of three or best of five. Hakim laughed. "Best of five, and if I don't win the next game then best of seven."

Oksanna smiled, stood and stretched. She walked to the door and leaned against the jamb, staring into darkness.

The phone rang. Nikos answered in Greek.

"Are you alright?" Victor asked, joining Oksanna.

"I'm happy right now. Imagine. Happy. And you, are you okay?"

"I think so."

"Frustrated?"

"Is it obvious?"

"You shouldn't compete with Nikos."

"I'm not."

"He's much younger than you."

"So?"

"And maybe better informed."

"He can be younger and better informed and still get it wrong."

She tilted her head. "Why compete?"

"I don't believe I'm part of a decaying empire that won't change, can't change. Do you agree with Nikos? Does Hakim?"

"Yes, of course. Although Hakim and Nikos argue about everything else."

"Like?"

"Hakim says Nikos places too much faith in reason."

"Well good for Nikos. If not reason, what hope is there?"

"You have to ask Hakim if you want to understand his way of thinking."

"Do you understand it?"

"I think so." She paused, then added softly. "I know I love him."

Victor was stunned. "I thought you were with Nikos."

"I am, but since our last trip to Alexandria, I'm with both."

Victor turned to look at the two men in the café. They were talking easily. He liked how their relationship appeared – open and frank. "Why isn't there tension between them?"

"You don't see any?"

"No."

"Maybe this trip has brought them closer."

"You think that or they think that?"

"We all think that."

Victor didn't know what to say. He concentrated on why he was there. "We haven't talked about Mahfouz."

"Nikos is working his contacts. That's why he's on the phone."

"But it's late!"

She laughed. "His night has just begun."

"How can he start without more information?"

"Nikos is a researcher. He looks at a problem and thinks process. He knows you and your lawyer are doing the obvious, but you asked him to find a different way. He's been texting people he trusts asking how to find a young Arab-Canadian missing in Cairo, perhaps imprisoned. That's what you wanted – isn't it? – a better way forward."

Victor was startled. He had thought he would remain at the centre of a slow, painstaking, person-to-person process, yet someone like Nikos, at home with digital media and the groupings it rapidly formed, might take the process far beyond his reach.

Oksanna noticed his hesitation. "Didn't you ask for his help?"

"I did."

"Do you still want it?"

"Of course."

CHAPTER THREE

T HE FOLLOWING EVENING Victor walked to Le Corniche and stood staring at the Mediterranean. A band of water thirty meters out caught his attention. The waves flattened leaving a smooth, luminous, grey-green surface, reminding him of polished jade. Strange, water like stone.

He approached the wall and looked down to where the waves met the garbage-strewn rocks. He could make out distinct swirls of pale green and dirty brown in the roiling. As he lifted his gaze the colours fused into the unexpected hue. Higher still, the sea transitioned into the more familiar indigo. At the furthest limit he saw a strip of pale mauve dispersing upwards. He watched as it thickened. He had never seen anything quite like it: a lavender sky spreading above water both indigo and jade.

To his right there was a tall man with a long fishing pole. He thought of Hans. As a boy he'd been astonished how fast he needed to run to keep up with the tall man's strides. Once, trying to stay abreast, he had stumbled and fallen into fresh snow. Hans had turned and laughed, then pushed open the rolling doors to the garage, exposing the colony's van raised on a hoist, its four wheels dangling.

Hans had set to work, removing the left-front wheel and rolling it away, returning to open the hub and remove the spindle. He turned and placed an object in the boy's hand. Victor still remembered the cold weight, his fingers stretching to get a better grip. It took him years to fully grasp the genius of a tapered roller bearing – minimizing each point of contact while setting the whole configuration spinning – but even in that moment he had intuited its strange power. He started to drift less often to the fields with their crops, or to the barns with their animals, but increasingly entered the repair shop where secrets were unveiled and Hans was the master.

Each object had a task for which it was specifically designed. Friction, avoided at all costs in certain circumstances, offered salvation in others. Victor learned the inverse relation of roller bearings to brake pads and callipers. Electricity, too, became real under Hans' tutelage. The spark that jumped at the end of the plugs ignited fuel in the piston in a process called combustion. Repeated at astonishing speeds, combustion built the compression that drove the crankshaft which delivered the torque which turned the axles upon which the wheels were fastened. It wasn't only bearings, brake pads, callipers, plugs, pistons and crankshaft which existed – this he knew for a certainty as he held each in turn – so too were the invisible forces for which they had been designed: friction, electricity, compression and torque.

Over a number of years Hans taught Victor that the vehicle, in its parts and as a unity, was a sustained conversation with the laws of nature. These laws could be relied upon because they never changed. One could place one's faith in them. In fact, it was suicidal not to. Such laws, however, were not the same as the invisible laws his father claimed real and unchanging. Not at all. His father warned Victor that this pride in mechanics – that was the word he always used, never accomplishment, ability, or facility – was blinding him to his deficiencies, spiritual in nature.

His mother hadn't wanted her son to leave the colony. She had spoken out on his behalf. But even she, over time, gave way to the father's steady pressure, eventually agreeing that departure was the precondition for an eventual return. For reasons Victor was never able to clarify, that didn't occur. If there had been a moment ripe with reconciliation, he missed it.

He stopped walking, resentful of memories that still stung. No reason to cling. He'd found independence and a different path forward. He was fortunate to have a life partner from outside the colony, fortunate to have his daughter and granddaughter. It was unimaginable, a life without Arden and the joys of Elena and Sharon. He wouldn't trade them for the world. No, not for the world!

Raising his head to look around, he saw a grouping of curious buildings on the other side of the road. They were framed in steel and covered in glass. Unlike other obviously modern buildings these didn't soar. The largest, in fact, was wide, low and angled to face the sky. He remembered the disc-shaped design from a magazine photograph accompanied by an architect's statement. It represented the building as a rising sun pulling free from the horizon.

Victor had heard it said the world was entering a new dark age, perhaps the darkest, in which the human species, now armed with appropriately destructive weapons and habits, clung to the grim intention of its own eradication. Yet here on a warm evening in December the Library of Alexandria had newly arisen, its interior lights beckoning.

Timing his movements to match the thinning traffic, Victor jogged across the broad avenue. He realized he was at the back of the complex and not at the main entrance. Turning one corner and then another, he came upon a larger-than-life figure composed of sculpted stone fit together and braced behind by a slender steel beam. The face was disturbingly undefined, yet the eyes were deeply gouged. He peered into their brooding vacancies. Could this be the sculpture which Hakim had mentioned, the one pulled from the sea? Had the grit of ceaseless currents worn the face smooth while scouring the eye sockets?

A thick hedge hid the lower third of the figure. He approached and peered through the branches. Thighs of stone had been set on two steel columns. Seen in its entirety, the fragmented sculpture with modern bracing made a bold and provocative statement which someone had chosen to mute behind shrubbery.

Victor noticed a cross-legged beggar, head bowed, sitting in the recessed opening of a door just past the sculpture. He was swathed in pale green rags. With only the slightest of hesitations Victor reached into his pocket, found three Egyptian pounds, and stooped to put the bills on the ground. He said the first words that came to him. "I hope this helps. At least a bit." The beggar replied calmly in Arabic with words Victor couldn't understand, then reached with his right hand to feel for and secure the gift.

He raised his face. The left eye was entirely closed, the upper eyelid having fused with the cheek beneath. No ear on that side, just a small black hole where it had once been. The right ear, however, was a perfectly formed example of what the other side was missing, the right eye opened a slit. The shortened nose, the result of a surgeon's best effort, was above a grimacing hole with terse lips, misaligned brown teeth permanently visible. No chin to speak of, the cheeks and neck corrugated with scars. The left sleeve dangled empty.

Such a ravaged face. Such a broken body.

It wasn't the physical damage alone which shocked Victor. It was the evident calmness of the voice and the precision of his movement, indicating a mind clear and entire. How could such a mind endure its frame?

Disoriented, he stumbled away in the direction from which he came. When he realized he was retracing his steps he decided it hadn't been the right moment to visit the library. It would wait. He'd return when he had time. He began to walk with resolve, to put distance between himself and the green figure.

He couldn't, however, run from his thoughts. Did the man celebrate or curse his survival? Were his waking hours absorbed with recollections of a happy past or filled with the regret of a moment's inattention? Was it absurd to wonder if, at the end of each day, he returned to the respect and affection of children who loved him? Or might his children have perished in the same fateful event?

Victor didn't notice the blackening water, the darkening sky. He was surprised by the sudden appearance of the hotel. The tape still covered the elevator service button on the ground floor. He gazed up the stairwell to the light and, once started, mounted without slowing. He stopped in the empty reception area to catch his breath. He fished the key from his pocket and entered the room. He automatically undressed and tucked himself between the sheets. He turned to the wall and closed his eyes.

He awoke to steady breathing on his neck. Ever so slowly he turned onto his back, then managed a further turn to face her. He smiled in the darkness at the lined and drawn face he knew so well. He remembered the slight skew to her nose where it had been broken in her youth. He saw her thin lips twitch, her brow furrow. He reached out and with the palm of his hand very gently soothed her forehead. He continued this motion until her breathing was regular and full.

* * *

He awoke alone, daylight flooding the room.

He had often welcomed Arden's presence since her death, but a brief and imagined smile over a vanishing shoulder was one thing, quite another to lay beside her. He was appalled her presence had been so lifelike, each breath convincing, the feel of her skin so real. Yet he was thrilled, too.

Rarely during her last weeks on intravenous had Arden been entirely awake, and then not for long. She had been on an unfathomable all-encompassing dispersion into the unknown, her consciousness drawn like water through sand to an invisible place. His hopes, one day to the next, had been to minimize her pain; but how to accept that measure of success when it would be most completely achieved through her death? He had held her, not wanting to sleep, fearing she might slip away.

Before she died Arden told him she thought nothingness a sufficient reward. Those were her exact words, 'a sufficient reward'. He had struggled to understand. To him the universe was tumultuous and irrepressible: dandelions cracked the concrete sidewalk, an obstructed sun made visible the distant brilliance of a billion stars – the complete opposite of nothingness. There was no nothingness. There never was a nothingness. The fact that she was no longer alive wasn't a nothingness either. It was an overflowing, unending, unabated sorrow that made no sense.

He sat naked at the small desk, uncertain of the time. He didn't feel hungry so it couldn't be late. He opened his notebook and calmly wrote a capital A on a clean page. That was for Arden. Further down he wrote a capital H. He wondered if it referred to Hans or Hakim. Without asking himself why, he wrote the words "from the sea" beside it. The H must refer to Hakim, given his enthusiasm for all things underwater: ships, sculptures, cities, and the knowledge submerged with them.

He and Hans had once discussed whether humans evolved from fish, or at least from fish-like creatures in the sea. Evolution from primates hadn't seemed far-fetched. The similarities between apes and people were apparent. It was a humbling stretch, though, that all land animals evolved from single celled creatures in the water. The hurdle wasn't genetic mutations as a means of physical change, it was the inconceivable time scale assumed. For most individuals a year is a long time and ninety years a long life. To those who thought the Bible factual, God created the world six thousand years ago. Biological evolution insisted one accept changes accumulating over thousands of millions of years. It made laughable the concept of ancient societies at the dawn of writing, a mere five thousand years ago. Against the scale of biological change, all known societies were contemporary.

While it was possible that the 'H' and 'from the sea' referred to Hakim, it could also refer to Hans. Either. Or both. He circled the letter and drew two arrows to the words to better represent the possible interpretations.

He had lived with Arden about three years before their daughter was born. He wrote the number down. Three. Then it was another eleven years before she died. Eleven. But even after fourteen years – he didn't write down such an obvious sum – the relationship had been fresh, as if they were just beginning to build a life together. He hadn't had time to know her as completely as possible, whatever that might mean. It wasn't a number, he knew that. There had been another year between Arden's death and Elena becoming pregnant at the age of fifteen.

It hadn't occurred to him that would happen – his child having a child – but together they'd committed to the unexpected. He had worked hard to help her bring up a happy daughter. It was the best thing he had done, or perhaps would ever do.

He turned the page and began to draw the schematic of a limited slip differential. Allowing the wheels on opposite ends of a single axle to spin at different speeds was an interesting problem. He enjoyed the few moments it took to capture the delightfully simple solution. It was amazing, he thought, that among all those zipping about in cars very few could explain a differential. Inexplicable, except for the wide-eyed indifference to the way the world works.

He turned to yet another fresh page to draw the schematic of a torque biasing differential, a system more commonly used on European and Asian cars. There were always options, even when addressing natural laws. That was the point, in mechanics and evolution. He wondered how he could annotate that. Was there a symbol he could use?

The phone rattled to life on the small desk beside him. With surging emotion he called out his daughter's name as he answered. "Elena!"

There was a pause.

"Victor?" The distinct English accent was immediately recognizable.

"Perpetua?"

"Yes."

"When I answered I was hoping … I'm sorry, my daughter is the only one who ever calls. I'm surprised to hear from you."

"Are you still in Alexandria?"

"I am. I don't know why I'm here anymore … in any case, I haven't left."

"Can you come to the office? There's a girl here who met Mahfouz."

"I'm sorry?"

"She recognized him. As soon as she saw the poster she told me his name. She wanted to know how I came to have his picture in my office."

"Can I meet her?"

"That's why I'm calling."

"I'd like to meet her soon."

"How about now? Is that possible?"

"My God, don't let her get away!"

"She doesn't want to get away. She wants to meet you. You'll need a translator and I can do that."

"I'll be there as soon as I can. Thank you. Thank you."

Victor struggled to his feet. He wished he'd already shaved, that his rinsed-out underwear on the sill had miraculously dried, that this moment was less of a blur.

CHAPTER FOUR

S HE TURNED HER FACE AWAY as Perpetua introduced her. "Fadumah lived in Daadab before coming to Egypt."

"Oh," Victor replied, not understanding. "Daadab? Where is that?"

"Kenya. It's a refugee camp in the north. At least three hundred and fifty thousand people are there, might be closer to half a million by now, mainly Somali. Fadumah is Somali."

The city in which Victor lived, an urban centre of some heft on the prairies, the second-largest city in the geographically diverse and sprawling province of Manitoba, had 50,000 people. When he moved there he thought it crowded. He tried to imagine a refugee camp with ten times as many.

"She's very young," he said, stating the obvious.

"Eighteen. Not a child. After her father was killed she and her mother decided to get her younger brothers out of the country. They put them on a boat to Italy."

"Her father was killed?"

"She said he died a martyr."

"And her brothers are in Italy," Victor repeated, to show he was listening.

"No, they didn't get there. Their boat was boarded before it left Egyptian waters. The passengers, mostly illegal migrants, are being held here in Alexandria. That's why she came. She hopes to see her brothers. I'm hoping she doesn't."

"I don't understand."

"Her presence, too, is illegal. It won't take the authorities long to figure that out. If she goes she'll join her brothers in detention."

Victor looked to Fadumah who was still looking away, then returned his gaze to Perpetua. "Is this the kind of case you usually handle?"

"It's one of a number of patterns. There's a constant stream of people trying to move through Egypt who never make it out. You'd think it a problem with a solution: they want out and the country doesn't want to keep them. Greece seems close, Italy close enough, there are ways to get them there … but neither country is willing to accept them."

"At least they didn't drown in the crossing," Victor said. "I'm happy her brothers are safe. Can you tell her that?"

Perpetua translated. The girl nodded slightly, as if acknowledging a formality. She began to ask questions.

"She would like to know if you're Canadian, like Mahfouz?"

"I am, yes."

"She wants to know if you like it there."

"Yes, I do."

"You think it a good place?"

"I don't know any other."

"Is that your answer?"

"I like it there," Victor affirmed. "I think most do."

"Is it racist?"

"Did she ask that?"

"She asked if people dislike Muslims."

"There are intolerant people, but the great majority accept Muslims."

"She asked ... she wants to know ... if you can get her brothers into Canada."

"I wouldn't know where to start."

"She asks if you'll try."

Victor appealed to Perpetua. "How can I answer that? I haven't thought about it."

"Simply tell her you're surprised and need to think it over."

"I came here hoping to learn about Mahfouz. Are there things she can tell me about him? Or is she saying she'll only help me find Mahfouz if I help her brothers?"

"She didn't say that. She's concerned for her brothers. She wants them to have a safe place to go."

Fadumah again asked questions.

"She wants to know if Mahfouz's father hired you. She thinks you must have special skills, otherwise the father would have come himself."

"I have no special skills. I'm here because my daughter and Mahfouz's mother asked me to come. They hope I can at least locate him."

Fadumah grew pensive and stopped speaking. She lowered her hands into her lap and looked at Victor with what he took to be a troubled expression. Then she looked away.

It was Perpetua who continued. "Where is Mahfouz's father?"

"In prison in Montreal."

"You didn't tell me that at our first meeting. Why is he there?"

"He was picked up on a Security Certificate. It can be issued without a specific charge or evidence of a crime. But it's not the father we're worried about. At least we know for certain where he is. But Mahfouz … it's not just that he's missing, or might be imprisoned, it's that …" He stopped abruptly, not wanting to speak his next thought.

"Would the Canadian government accept the torture of one of its citizens?" Perpetua asked, filling in the blank.

"There are known cases of the government providing information to interrogators torturing Canadians abroad."

"As part of the so-called war on terror?"

"Yes." Victor was grateful to her. Back home these topics, if approached at all, were spoken of in polite fits and starts, the facts put in doubt. Avoiding hard issues didn't seem Perpetua's way.

"Why is the father in prison?" she asked.

"Because of the son. They're looking for evidence to implicate both."

"What kind of evidence?"

"A government lawyer told us Mahfouz gave money to a man in Cairo with terrorist connections."

Perpetua turned to Fadumah and again translated. Agitated, Fadumah shifted in her seat, leaned forward, spoke with anger.

"She wants to know if you're blaming her father for what happened?"

"Did Mahfouz give money to her father?"

Fadumah's words, slow to start, gathered force. Her hands came to life, darting forward to emphasize the accumulating points. Perpetua reached out to still their whirling but the girl moved to avoid her. Her eyes sought out and peered directly into Perpetua's gaze, then at Victor. Her words hesitated, suddenly stopped.

Perpetua grunted from deep in her throat, encouraging her to continue.

The girl responded with quick shallow gasps. Tears fell without restraint, washing her face. A whole new range of sounds and rhythms streamed out of her mouth in compact density. Victor realized she must be speaking Somali. With a look of anxiety the girl spoke again in Arabic, translating herself. She began to go back and forth in both languages until, filled with frustration, she clenched her eyes shut, tightly folded her arms across her chest, angled her face towards the floor and went silent.

Perpetua waited several moments in absolute stillness, then rose and left the room.

Victor and Fadumah were alone. It wasn't awkward between them. Nothing was needed other than for each to act politely indifferent to the other, which they did.

The minutes lengthened.

Perpetua re-entered holding a small cardboard box. She put it down and fussed with crockery and cutlery as she spoke to Fadumah. Not long after there was a cup of tea and a small piece of cake with a fork in front of each of them. Settling into her seat Perpetua turned to Victor. "I should have started with tea and cake. That's one of the worthwhile things I learned from the English."

"Will you tell me what she said?"

"She said many things."

"Does any of it concern me?"

"Yes, but give me a minute. I need to sort it out. Please, eat."

The three sipped tea and ate cake.

"I'll tell you what I learned. Her father wanted to buy a fragrance store to support his family. He asked a friend, Ibrahim, for financial help. It was he who suggested that although he didn't have the money he would ask his brother who had a successful business in Montreal. Not long after the brother's son, Mahfouz, came to Cairo. There was an event to welcome him. Her whole family went, her brothers, her mother, her father; they were all there. She told me it was a happy day. Her father delivered a small speech and Mahfouz stood to give his reply. He spoke well. Everyone was hopeful. That was the only time she met Mahfouz."

"The once?"

"Yes."

"Yet she recognized him right away when she saw his picture on your wall …"

"Was she wrong?"

"No."

"She also said her father had told her Mahfouz was considering marrying her."

Victor was stunned. He didn't understand how such a statement was possible. He turned to her and asked in English, as if she would miraculously understand, "Why do you think Mahfouz wanted to marry you?"

Perpetua translated. Fadumah replied and Perpetua again translated. "Mahfouz never said anything. Only her father had. She was wrong to have listened to him."

Victor realized he would never know the true situation. All he had to go on was Perpetua's summarizing translation. That would have to be sufficient. He remembered why he was in her office. "Does she know where Mahfouz is now?"

"She doesn't know."

"If she had to guess?"

"She says he might be in prison, or perhaps he too fell a martyr, like her father."

"Why does she call her father a martyr?"

"There was a second meeting in the store. Just the men. When her father didn't return she went to look for him. The police had covered the shattered windows of the store with brown paper and taped shut the door. She was later told that her father died inside. Perhaps Mahfouz was killed at the same time."

"Who told her that?"

"The man she works for."

"Who is he? How would he know?"

The women again conferred.

"He sells used appliances: stoves, fridges, washing machines, dryers. Fadumah cleans them as they come in. She's not sure how he knew. Maybe through the Ihkwan."

"The Muslim Brotherhood?"

"That is how her boss met Ibrahim."

"He has no idea what happened to Mahfouz?"

"He, too, would like to know."

"How can someone just disappear?"

"It happens all the time," Perpetua answered. "In my experience there's usually a trace. It starts in the holding cells. They can be crowded – thirty or more in a space designed for six. Everyone talks. Someone saw him. Someone asked him questions. But how to find that someone?"

Victor hesitated. "Would Fadumah introduce me to this man, her boss?"

"Are you sure you want to get involved?"

"That's why I'm here."

"Fadumah's father fought for the Union of Islamic Courts in Somalia. That fact alone makes him a terrorist in the eyes of the Egyptian government."

"I know nothing about that."

"I doubt Mahfouz did either. He went to a first meeting and everything was fine, but during or after the second meeting he was picked up for reasons he couldn't possibly understand."

"All I want to do is locate a young Canadian who has been wrongly imprisoned. The Egyptian state is not threatened by someone like me."

Perpetua stared at him in silence. "Mahfouz is dark-skinned and Arabic. You're white and a foreigner. You're wrong if you think the difference will protect you."

"I don't think that."

"You assume it. But if you want me to ask the question I will."

Victor nodded and the interchange between the two women was short.

"She said if you go to Cairo she will introduce you to him."

"Please thank her."

Perpetua did so, then placed her hand gently over Fadumah's.

"At the end," Victor said, "just before she stopped, she seemed in great pain. What was she saying?"

"She was talking to me at that point. Not you. I don't have to translate everything."

"What did she say?"

"She said she no longer believed in Allah, and that was why he had abandoned her." Perpetua stood to gather the tea cups and small plates, ending the conversation.

Victor, irritated by what he took to be Perpetua's indifference, wanted to explain that he, too, felt abandoned by a God who no longer existed. The disappearance of an omnipotent father had been easy to accept – it caused no pain – but that there would never be divine justice, none at all … that had been difficult.

He remembered being saddened and euphoric in turn in a series of conquests – or what he thought were conquests – young women attracted to the raw physicality of an exiled farm boy. He had made sense of it by closing his eyes and claiming freedom. Any act which gained advantage over another was the virtue of the day. All he had known was the self-interest and cynicism which held the city together. The sacred disappeared.

It was Arden, after those lost years, who allowed the particularities of goodness to again emerge. She showed him how they might weave a fragile yet ethical abode, building a small and serviceable home into which they could introduce a beloved child.

And now there were two empty bedrooms at home.

"I'll help her brothers," he suddenly said, shifting to the back of his seat and sitting straight.

"Are you sure?"

"I've never done anything like it so I'll need time to put the pieces in place. I don't even know what the pieces are, but you'll help me, won't you?"

"If I can."

"Tell her I may not succeed in getting them into Canada, but I'll try."

As the translation sank in, Fadumah's tight lips broke into a series of flickering smiles.

* * *

He walked to Le Corniche and, initially distracted, once again found himself gazing at the calm Mediterranean. He was beginning to like this now familiar view.

There are undercurrents, he thought, not seen with the eye nor heard with the ear. They ripple ceaselessly in all directions, shaping us despite our ignorance, gifting the unexpected. Going into the meeting he had known nothing of Fadumah, let alone of her brothers, and certainly not that he might assume responsibility for them.

The boys were in Alexandria, not far away, their futures entangled with his. They had been drawn together because Fadumah had recognized Mahfouz's face, because Perpetua had allowed him to put a poster on the wall, because he had come to Egypt, because his daughter had moved to Montreal and there met a young man with whom she shared hopeful smiles, incomplete conversations, physical intimacies, transforming historical possibilities into personal commitments.

He was willing to stake his life on helping his daughter and this was the way to do it. It had led him here among these people. His way forward was to be sensitive to their requests, to help them when possible while making his own needs known. He was on the ethical path. To abandon it would be to betray those he loved. If he did that the world would crumble.

THE SECOND GATE

Montreal

2009

CHAPTER FIVE

Entering at the back of the raked lecture hall, Elena overlooked descending semi-circular rows of wooden chairs each with a small writing surface attached. People were already gathered, having muted conversations in dispersed clusters, filling a third of a room designed for four hundred. The lights were dim, except directly over the podium, where a spotlight shone.

Feeling uneasy and alone in a foreign space, unsure what to expect, she chose a seat near where she entered on the outside aisle. She had hoped to recognize someone, perhaps a friend of Mahfouz's, but saw no one she knew.

If the event was important, shouldn't the room be full?

She tried to recall what she knew of the war in Iraq. Not much. There were certain images: a giant Saddam Hussein, hand high in the air, a thick chain fastened around his neck. The sequence had played over and over on screens everywhere: the chain pulled taut, tauter, tauter still until the sculpture cracked at the knees, broke at the feet, and fell. The sculpture falling, the regime fallen. The pictures of Saddam's dead sons also everywhere, faces swollen, bloody, bruised. She remembered, too, that image of the American president on an aircraft carrier facing cheering sailors row upon row beneath a huge sign, 'Mission Accomplished'.

Then – was it on YouTube? – images captured by a cell phone in a dark room. Men dressed in black, faces covered, placing a thick rope around a neck and Saddam falling down, now a corpse at the end of a noose. It felt odd watching the death of a person on her computer screen. She wondered if the clip was still available.

Exactly on the hour a small woman with handsome features, dark hair, dark eyes, and a modest headscarf, walked up to the podium. She appeared to be in her late forties. Elena didn't know if she were the speaker or someone to make the introductions. It occurred to her that she didn't actually know the gender of the speaker, having assumed it would be male.

The woman at the podium checked her watch, tapped the small black microphone. The muttering ceased. There was a moment of silent expectation, catching Elena by surprise.

"More snow is expected. For those of you who drove I thank you for your effort getting here. For those who took Montreal's wonderful metro system – you and I don't face the challenge of driving home. I hope a few more people will straggle in so, if no one minds, I'll wait a few minutes for latecomers." The speaker stepped away from the microphone, stood in profile, head bowed, in a moment of reflection.

Elena watched as a young couple entered, books in hand, followed by an older woman wearing a fuchsia beret and matching scarf, reminding her of Rachel. It had never occurred to her that Rachel might attend. But was it her? The couple chose a place near the front and the single woman sat in the row behind them.

The speaker straightened and turned square to the microphone. "It's a fact that actions taken against the people of Iraq

since 1990 meet the legal criteria of genocide. These premed-
itated actions were initiated and insisted upon by the governments of the United States and the United Kingdom and
endorsed by the United Nations Security Council. It follows
that the leaders of the United States, the United Kingdom and
the United Nations who condoned those actions should be
charged with the crime."

Elena was surprised: mostly by the softness of the tone
in which the words were delivered. She sounded unhurried,
relaxed, sure of herself.

"I'm often asked why I'm not grateful to the United States
for removing Saddam Hussein from power. The answer to that
will become clear as the evening continues. Let me just say,
to start, that despite whatever problems and shortcomings my
country had, Iraq was, until recently, a beacon of modern sec-
ular development in the Middle East. It had well-functioning
systems of public education and public health, available to
everyone and universally free. It made no difference if you were
Shia or Sunni, Christian or Communist; well-supplied well-
organized schools and hospitals welcomed you. There was a
very high rate of literacy and strong representation of women in
the workplace. The universities of Iraq, thought to be the best
in the Middle East, had a high percentage of women students.
That is not the case today, six years after the invasion. Not at all.

"I understand that many of you will not want to believe me.
Facts, however, support me, and will continue to do so unless
– or is it until? – our history is rewritten to suit Western narratives. That process has begun. It's evident in English, French
and German sources. I expect a more true record to be maintained primarily in Arabic, Farsi, Russian and, I hope, Chinese."

She paused, began again. "What I'm trying to achieve tonight is an informed conversation that stays on topic. While

many people I once knew are no longer alive, I'm not here to seek justice for them. They can't hear what I say and nothing I do will affect them. There are millions who fled Iraq. The great majority did not find foreign countries in which to settle. They live as refugees in countries that do not want them. Others have returned to our national ruins. They, and those who never left, live under foreign occupation in the midst of an on-going civil war. I will not repeat their individual stories of suffering, however numerous and moving. There are well-known groups who specialize in the anecdotal. They have glossy photos and well edited videos that accompany heart-wrenching appeals. What they don't have are the facts to help you understand what happened and why. They want to engage your pity, or your guilt, to pry open your pockets. That doesn't interest me. I will tell you the number of children killed by the sanctions but I won't show pictures of them. There is a large screen behind me, but it will remain rolled up. If anyone is here to enjoy an act of public catharsis, they will be disappointed. I have reasons for personal anger and outrage, but in my experience emotional appeals derail the needed discussion.

"No one in this room is responsible for the implementation of the West's genocidal policies. There are such people. They exist. They are elsewhere, enjoying honours given for the crimes they committed. I know that for a fact because I know who they are: to begin, the members of the Office of Special Plans, a working group set up in the heart of the US administration specifically to plan and implement the war against Iraq. We have their names, and can show how the mainstream media partnered with them, printing false information as news and writing compelling editorials based on this deception. The existence of hidden weapons of mass destruction is the most obvious lie, but far from the only one.

"When I state that the treatment of Iraq is a case of genocide, I am usually met by loud cries insisting that can't possibly be true. When I ask why not, the same two reasons are always given. The first, rarely stated this succinctly: not enough Iraqis died. The second: there was never any intent to destroy the people of Iraq and since intent must exist for genocide, it didn't happen.

"Let's discuss the numbers issue first. To date it's estimated – in my mind conservatively – that at least one-and-a-half million Iraqis died due to recent sanctions, bombings, invasion and occupation. I hope you'll agree that a million and a half is a significant number. However, before we get lost in the controversy of numbers – and there is always a controversy around numbers – I want to clarify that it's not the number of dead which determines genocide.

"Assume I have, or had, seven brothers and sisters. In fact, that's true, you don't have to assume it. I was born one of eight children. Now if someone were to kill one of my siblings it would be hard for me to make the case that my whole family was threatened. The first death could be a one-off, an isolated incident. I'd have better grounds if a second sibling died, yet it would still be hard to mount a convincing case. However, if I uncover plans to kill my brothers and sisters as well as myself, and the manner of death of both siblings fits the plan, wouldn't I have a right to say that the eradication of my family is intended, and that there is evidence of the policy's implementation? The fact that five of my brothers and sisters remain alive is a blessing. It doesn't disprove intent. There are many who don't grasp this. They argue it's foolish to pay attention to my paranoid exaggerations, preferring – in fact demanding – that the topic not be raised until it can be definitively shown that I and my siblings are all dead. Only then will there be sufficient evidence to evaluate the claim."

There was dispersed laughter in the room. Elena felt too awkward to join in.

"You laugh! Good! You should laugh! It is an absurd argument made in bad faith. It is designed to prolong the agony of a targeted population at its most vulnerable."

The lecturer turned her head slowly from one side to the other, as if momentarily elsewhere, recalling someone's absence.

"To the second point. Many are willing to call what happened in Iraq a mistake, even a tragic mistake. They go on to say it was the unexpected result of the best intentions. Certainly it was tragic, but a crime, not a mistake. As the years go by and the crimes accumulate, it doesn't take much reflection to grasp that those who made the decisions were never as ignorant and naïve as their apologists claim. It became clear years ago that those who determined policy lied to the public about what they were doing and why they were doing it. Let me ask: Is there anybody in this room, anyone at all, surprised to hear that the British and American governments lie?"

Again there was laughter. This time, Elena joined in.

"Most of you will have heard that half a million Iraqis below the age of five died due to sanctions imposed prior to the invasion. It is impossible for either the American or British government to claim they didn't know about this, two top administrators within the United Nations resigned, one after the other, each publicly stating the sanctions were genocidal. That is the term they used, putting it on record. The American Secretary of State accepted this number in a recorded interview. She claimed it was 'worth it'. Madeleine Albright accepted the lives of children as an acceptable currency and half a million as a reasonable price.

"My question: a price for what? We are told that the deaths were necessary to stop weapons of mass destruction. Okay, but what was the relationship between the one and the other? Were children under five building the weapons? You can tell me that's a silly question, but I say it cuts to the chase. If someone initiates an action knowing it will not give them the result they say they are seeking, then what they say is a lie. What they know they are getting is what they want. The death of Iraqi children through sanctions is what the American and British authorities were getting, and it is what they wanted, evidenced by maintaining the policies which achieved it. They decided to destroy the people of my country beginning with the easiest targets, the most vulnerable, the children.

"They also decided to attack and destroy our national culture and history. Let me give an example. Rare books are easy to hide, to transport, to sell. They are also worth a lot of money. Looters don't burn rare books. They steal them. Yet during the invasion many hundreds of our most precious and valuable books weren't stolen, which would make sense, but were burned, which doesn't. Traces of fire accelerants were found in the national library proving the burnings were intentional. This means the criminals who intentionally started fires were getting paid. Who was paying these thugs to destroy the treasures of Iraq? Who made the lists of culturally important books to destroy? Was it the same people who refused to send guards to protect the treasures in the Museum of Antiquities in Baghdad, despite the frantic urging of archeologists, librarians and historians from around the world? The damage to thousands of important cultural artefacts of Sumerian, Akkadian and Babylonian culture was astonishing, as much for its specific targeting as for its thoroughness.

"Should I mention that the American army chose to set a military base directly on the archeological site of one of Nebuchadnezzar's ancient palaces. Why would anyone choose to park the steel treads of 21st century tanks on handmade bricks from 2600 years ago? Was it profound ignorance or was it – in someone's mind – a righteous act of revenge against those who built the palace during the Babylonian Empire?

"Maybe you believe what I see as a pattern is simply the result of incoherent and random activities. Stuff happens. If so, are you also willing to believe one-by-one assassinations of at least three hundred and fifty leading scientists and academics a remarkable string of random acts?"

"Those in the hard sciences were the first to be targeted: physics, chemistry, engineering. Among those killed were my eldest brother, a chemist, and one of my younger brothers, a professor of computer programming. They were murdered three weeks apart, each while leaving home, both with the efficiency of a professional hit. Most think it was the work of the Mossad, which claims the right to assassinate any Arab or Iranian scientist anywhere. If by the Mossad then with the blessing of the CIA. Frankly, in our part of the world, it's impossible to tell the one from the other. Although the killers remain anonymous and will never be brought to justice, I want to say that the victory of the dead is that they were known, loved, and will not be forgotten. Colleagues and students mourn them. Partners and children mourn them. I mourn them."

Elena had been profoundly shocked when she first grasped the reality of Mahfouz's disappearance in Cairo. A sense of impotent panic overwhelmed her. But given the official response – indifference to his fate by both Egyptian and Canadian governments – her panic had transformed into a gnawing despair with intermittent outbreaks of confused anger. When she tried to soothe her spirit, she discovered her heart was burning, a glowing coal smoldering painfully at the core of her being. She imagined the pain would eventually end, but only when her heart turned to ash. This woman in front of her was not raging. Or weeping. Her voice was not trembling. Was her heart already ash?

The speaker continued. "How much proof is necessary before it is accepted that a choice was made to destroy the Iraqi people – future, past and present? Despite that desire to erase the tenses of our existence, I want to assure you that Iraq will be rebuilt. The murdering of one generation will not be enough. The murder of a second generation is ongoing and, I assume, plans to kill future generations are being developed. They, too, will not be enough. We survived the century-long barbarism of the Mongol invasion and will survive the century-long barbarism of the Anglo-American invasions."

Elena wanted to question this confidence. How could she predict across generations? How could she sustain long-term objectives? How was that confidence achieved? Did her heart burn cool to conserve the passions needed?

She remembered Rachel telling her she was chaff. Fluff. Not exactly those words, but it is what she meant. She had said that if you don't know who you are then you don't have an identity, if you don't have an identity the winds will toss you about. You will land wherever and whenever the wind drops you.

So who was she? Female? White? Christian? Canadian? Were they her essence? Then this person in front – female, yes, but not white, not Christian, not Canadian – was she essentially different? It didn't seem so. Not at all.

The lecturer paused, drank water, peered again into the darkness in front of her. She picked up and slowly waved a collection of stapled pages. "At the end of the evening I will give each of you a bullet list of facts shared tonight with their sources. I have enough copies for everyone. In fact, I have enough for the seats that are empty, too, so please feel free to take as many as you want. Share your copies with friends or colleagues, anyone who might be interested. Most importantly, if you can prove a fact wrong, or point to an unreliable source, email me. I will look into it and respond. I'm confident that the give and take of honest criticism will strengthen my case, not weaken it, that this document can get stronger each time it is presented."

* * *

The lighting brightened during a smattering of courteous applause. The taut energy at the beginning of the lecture had dissipated. No one expected further revelations. The lecturer had held court for an hour and a half, never raising her voice, in a room that listened with varying degrees of comprehension, interest and irritation. She announced she'd take questions.

The first to the microphone was a stocky young man in his early thirties. He wanted clarification on the numbers of dead. Why was she talking in the millions? Were her sources reliable? It had to be asked – don't shoot the messenger – but wasn't everything she had just said anti-American propaganda?

The speaker held up her fact sheet, assuring everyone that the numbers were up-to-date and reliable. They were, she said, figures that came from America itself, not the US government, of course, but independent scholars. They were provided by the MIT Center for International Studies, revised a month ago. She had no reason to believe the Center had any anti-American bias.

The young man ceded the microphone to a thin, wiry, grey-haired man. He shifted from foot to foot, introduced himself as Jewish but not Zionist. He wanted to know why, so soon after the horrors of Cast Lead and the massacres in Gaza, the speaker didn't address the role of Israel in the foreign policy of the UK and the USA? How could one discuss the invasion of Iraq without discussing the role of Israel?

"I expected this question," the speaker replied. "No matter who or what shaped the foreign policies of the US and the UK, they were the policies of the US and the UK. Agreed? They were by far the leading nations, although strongly supported by Australia and Poland who also sent soldiers. I don't want the necessary conversation about what they did in Iraq to be pulled off-track by a conversation about Israel. I hope that's possible."

The man at the microphone continued to shuffle, but didn't respond.

An intense young woman, only slightly older than Elena, wanted to know why it was so important to establish genocide as the crime. What purpose did it serve?

The lecturer thanked the young woman for the question. She agreed it would be simpler to speak of war crimes and crimes against humanity, neither of which needed proof of intent for conviction. She noted that the laws regarding genocide reflected a legal concept developed after the Second World War. It was too early to know if, in practice, they would further justice or become an impediment, as crimes get lost in interminable arguments about motives. For example, some claimed that reconstruction monies earmarked to rebuild Iraq proved the actions not genocidal. Yet such reconstruction contracts provide opportunities for corruption on a truly staggering scale. Often all the money went out but the project was only partially realized. Should we believe, she asked, that after-the-fact corruption disproves genocide?

The young woman protested that she hadn't addressed the question. She repeated it. Why was it important to prove genocide?

The lecturer paused a long time. Finally she answered. "If the leaders in Washington and London knew the results of what they were doing – and they did – and if those actions fit the legal definition, shouldn't they be charged?"

"You're pushing too far," the young women said. "You just confirm yourself as the enemy."

"How am I doing that?"

"Mistakes were made. Okay. Maybe certain things shouldn't have happened. But we are not evil. Our intentions are not evil. If you say they are, how can you be anything but an enemy?"

"I said nothing about evil. Nothing."

"You said what you said. I'm saying what I'm saying. You should know that we won't let you win. We can't let you win."

The young woman walked away from the microphone.

The lecturer was silent. "I want to thank you all for coming," she said softly, her energy flagging, her left hand resting on the fact sheets. "I hope this evening has been useful."

CHAPTER SIX

Elena was relieved to stand and stretch. She started to the front to pick up a fact sheet. She thought she would get three, one each for Josh and Ghadir. As she grew closer the woman in the fuchsia beret momentarily turned.

"I wondered if it was you," Elena said. "But I couldn't imagine you being here."

"I didn't expect to come. But I'm glad I did. It's good to get misinformation directly from the horse's mouth."

Elena continued down the remaining stairs to pick up the printed handouts, then rejoined Rachel.

"Why do you call it misinformation?"

"I'm sure many of her facts are right, but I don't like how she manipulates them."

"Because she calls it a genocide?"

"Why does she pretend Iraqis were hunted down like Jews during the Second World War? Who's she kidding?"

"Maybe not all genocides are the same."

"Maybe it's not genocide."

They exited the hall and stepped, side-by-side, onto the escalator. The floor-to-ceiling windows in front grew larger and larger as they descended, an expanding frame for the whirling snow in the glow of streetlights. They reached the main floor and headed towards a crowd milling near the exit where there was a general pulling on of hats and hoods, a donning of gloves and mittens.

"Would you like to go for a drink?" Rachel asked. "I owe you that."

"You paid me for all my shifts. You gave me two weeks notice. You don't owe me anything."

Rachel hadn't expected to be taken literally, but if the girl preferred to be precise, "I wasn't exactly honest when I fired you."

"I know that. You said it was because my French wasn't good enough. It was actually because Mahfouz was my boyfriend."

"Yes. I'm sorry. I was frightened"

"Why?"

"His father was accused of terrorism. I panicked. I wish I hadn't."

"You mean that?"

"Yes, I do. Do you have news about him?"

"We think he's in prison somewhere in Egypt."

"I'm sorry."

Elena considered the apology. "Thank you."

"And your daughter? I miss Sharon. How is she?"

The answer was restrained and cool. "She's fine."

"I guess I've lost you."

"As an employee? Yes. I have a job as a barista."

"I meant as a friend."

Elena wasn't surprised by the question. She, too, had once thought they were close. "I've always liked you, Rachel, and what you say has always had an effect on me."

Rachel was comforted by a statement she recognized as true. "Why don't we find a place to talk? Are you open to that?"

* * *

The establishments along Crescent Street reflected a casual luxury which intimidated Elena, but she was entering with a confident and worldly older woman. Rachel, invigorated by the brisk walk in the cold air, spoke effusively as she climbed the few steps towards a heavy wooden door. "Sometimes snow falls and it changes the world. Makes it beautiful. Look at the parked cars! Completely covered! It reminds me of *The Ballad of Narayama*." She held the door open for Elena. "You haven't a clue what I'm talking about, have you?"

"No."

"How could you? It's a Japanese film. I don't remember when it was made. Fifties? Sixties? Josh would know." Rachel's eyes adjusted. She saw an available table for two beneath an illuminated stained-glass window, not far from the working fireplace. She headed towards it.

"Does Josh know a lot about Japanese films?" Elena asked, settling into a comfortable chair with padded armrests.

"That's what he would like us to believe. Is he still lending you books?"

"No. I didn't read them. I disappointed him."

"You're in contact though?"

"Sometimes he calls. Not often."

Rachel nodded. It was as she suspected, he had moved on. Well, he never focused on one person for too long. "Does he have anyone in his life?"

"I don't know, but Rachel, should you care?"

"You're right! You're right! I left him! I moved out! I don't care! You said you're working?"

"Mornings. Drip coffees to go. Not that exciting."

"It can't pay well, a barista.".

"Nothing at all the first few days. They said I was in training."

"You accepted that?"

"I figured if they didn't hire me afterwards at least I'd have a skill."

"If you consider pouring coffee a skill."

Elena replied in an oddly deadpan nasal voice. "You know, I tried to find somebody to teach me brain surgery – I really did – I asked everyone I knew. I even told them I'd bring the necessary tools: hammer, saw, pliers."

Rachel laughed. "You're good at that. Voices. But you're too sensitive, I'm not suggesting you're stupid. I'm not a brain surgeon either, am I?"

"Not. Even. Close," Elena said, emphasizing each word.

"Fuck you," Rachel replied good-naturedly.

"Rachel, you never swear!"

"I never used to, but I'm learning. Did it sound natural or a bit forced?"

"Natural."

"Good. I'm trying to drink more, too. A long way to go before I'm an honest drunk, but at least I'm becoming less predictable."

"Since when have you been predictable?"

"I take that as a compliment. Shall we order wine, or pretend it's summer and make it margaritas?"

"Margaritas!"

Rachel raised her hand. The server took the order.

"Are you living alone?" Elena asked.

"Not even a cat. It's good for me. I need to face up to the fact that I'm not a failure because I don't have a partner."

"I can't imagine you think yourself a failure."

"It drives me crazy, sadness wells up ... I feel emotionally empty. I hate it."

The salt encrusted glasses arrived. Elena held hers firmly. "I don't want you to think of me as fluff, Rachel. I was thinking about that during the lecture. I want you to know that I'm not fluff."

Rachel was taken aback. "I've never called you fluff. Or have I? I think you're young. Well, you are young, but that is, I assure you, a temporary crime."

"You told me if I didn't know who I was I'd get blown around."

"That's true, and it's not only you. We all need anchors."

"We do?"

"To stay rooted, to counter the drift."

"You just said you wanted to be less predictable. How are you going to be less predictable while attached to an anchor?" Elena raised her glass and emptied it in a series of quick gulps. She frowned as the alcohol hit her. She brought the empty glass down to the table with a loud click.

In reply Rachel raised her glass and downed it the same way. She also frowned as she brought the glass down with a loud click. "You know," she said, "if we want to drink this way we should order the tequila straight."

"Show me how."

Rachel again raised her hand. The server took the order for two shooters each.

"You said you hadn't expected to see me tonight," Rachel said. "Do you think I'm stupid and want to remain so?"

"That's not how I see you."

"Good. I went to the lecture for the same reason you did, to understand what's happening. Or at least what people say is happening."

The liquid gold arrived in small transparent glasses. Rachel put salt on the back of her hand. Elena followed. Rachel licked the salt, as did Elena. They downed the liquor simultaneously, both happy with the success of the simple ritual.

"I haven't thought about that film for a while," Rachel said. "*The Ballad*. It moved me when I first saw it. It begins with a theft of potatoes from a storage area. That doesn't seem like a big deal, a few stolen potatoes. But the theft happens again. Not long after, in the middle of the night, the villagers attack a family and drag them from their beds. They force adults and children, all half asleep, into a pit and begin to shovel dirt on top of them. The family struggles to get out but they're pushed back. Eventually they are entirely covered, but the earth continues to move. The villagers keep shovelling. Then, somehow, the hole is filled. The pit no longer exists. The dead have disappeared, as has the means of killing them."

"The family is buried alive?"

"Because the father was a thief."

"But the whole family is punished?"

"Killed, not punished. Culled. Cleansed from the community. Their empty hut taken over the next day by a young couple. The teapot hadn't even cooled before it was being held in different hands."

"Sad."

"It's how history works."

"Is it?"

"The strong kill the weak. It's what the lecture was about."

"It was?"

"Iraq was using its oil wealth to get stronger. It made perfect sense for Iraq's enemies to act quickly, not later. It was rational to destroy the country as soon as possible. Do you know the saying 'If someone is coming to kill you, rise against him and kill him first'?"

"You're confusing me."

"You may be confused, Elena, but it's not me doing it. The weak die in the dark and are quickly forgotten. That's reality. How did she put it: past, present and future denied. I thought she got that part right. But the film I'm talking about isn't about the family being buried alive, that's just background. Context. It's about a mother who decides she's a burden to her family, one mouth too many in a family with too little. So she tells her son she wants him to carry her up the mountain to die. That's what they did with old people. They didn't put them in a home for the aged and then stop payments. They carried them up a mountain and left them there. The son refuses. He points out she's in good health and has all her teeth."

"Good for him."

"She knocks her front teeth out."

"She doesn't!"

"She does. The son finally agrees and the day arrives. The mother fits herself into a sling on his back. She tells him they can't talk. He starts up the path, begins to sweat, to struggle, but keeps going. Higher and higher. They pass the corpses of old people who weren't carried all the way to the top. It's gruesome: birds peck at skeletons, tear flesh from the more recently dead. The son is horrified. He doesn't want to leave his mother on the mountain. He turns to go back, but she hits him and points upward. He begins again. Struggles. It begins to snow. Like tonight it really comes down. It covers everything and … it's beautiful. The rotting bodies are hidden beneath gentle mounds of white. The world starts again, innocent and young. They reach the top. The mother slips out of the sling and waves her son away. He turns for a last look. She is sitting with a straight back among the rocks, meditating. The falling snow looks like a finely knitted shawl over her head, her shoulders."

"She's going to freeze to death."

"Yes."

"You support that?"

"It was her choice. She's found meaning in how she dies."

"What kind of meaning is that?"

"The strength to die gracefully, to leave the resources she no longer needs to her children."

Elena considered. "The mother sacrificed herself for her children, and nature recognized this as virtuous by snowing at exactly the right moment, proving without a doubt she made the right choice."

"Films are metaphors," Rachel said, happy to have explained it clearly.

"My god, Rachel, you're a wannabe martyr nagged by feelings of failure."

"When did I say I felt like a failure?"

"Not even fifteen minutes ago."

Rachel sighed, then asked with disarming honesty, "How can you remember that far back?"

Elena laughed. Rachel joined in.

"Besides, why be a martyr? No one would notice."

"Is being a martyr about being noticed?"

"Maybe not. Maybe not."

"Do you resent the fact I'm half your age?"

"You can let that thought go. Sometimes I wish I had used my early years better, but that's not the same thing."

"What would you do differently?"

"Have different expectations, be less naive."

"What does that mean, less naive?"

"Yeah, well, that's the problem. It's a long process, answering that question. This is what I think: if you do the right thing you don't end up living alone. So I did something wrong, but I don't know what it was.

"Aren't we all alone, fundamentally?"

"Sharon needs you. Ghadir needs you. Maybe your father needs you. When people need you, you're not alone."

"No one needs you?"

"My children have grown up, moved out, do what makes sense to them. They're independent. I'm glad about that. But no, they don't need me. I realize now that Josh never needed me."

"You're feeling sorry for yourself."

"I admit it." Rachel was silent for a moment. "Do you know what it's like to marry someone you love, only to discover he's incapable of loving you in return?"

"Josh is incapable of love?"

"I was smoldering when I left him. I needed to cool. Maybe I still do. I should have admitted years ago I was living with a narcissist. For some reason I refused to see it. Or I saw it and refused to believe it. Either way I clung to self-deception. That's depressing, don't you think? He used to tell me he was sorry for his infidelities. But he wasn't. Ever. He forgave himself again and again through self-centred pride. He told me his passions were so strong that they would have overwhelmed anyone. Imagine. Anyone! So not his fault. But the infidelities weren't the worst of it. I mean, they drained the trust out of our relationship, but worse than that, he wouldn't take my day-to-day struggles seriously. I had begun to hate myself. He considered it normal. It suited his needs. Maybe you don't understand, but I know other women that would."

"You managed to get out."

"At least that."

Rachel reached for her remaining glass. Elena did the same. They downed the shooters in unison, both exaggerating their grimace at the end, both clicking the glass hard on the table in shared victory.

"Josh always told me I should see myself objectively. Well, I wanted that, too ... but he meant I should see myself as he saw me, then I'd understand why he had priority. I gave into that. Not easily. Not right away. But slowly, step by step, over many years. For the longest time, even after being defeated, I clung to the hope that his love would deepen. Imagine waiting for a love that doesn't exist to deepen."

"I'm sorry."

"He knows my body. The physical object. He tells me, accurately, how it has changed over the years. But the inner maze which makes me who I am – my desires, will, experiences, feelings, thoughts – he refuses to meet me there. And I am quite interesting. At least ... I'm not *empty*."

"He's been nice to me."

"All narcissists are nice, especially at the beginning. They specialize in that kind of thing. You haven't slept with him have you ... because he's been nice?"

"Would it make a difference if I had?"

"Yes. No. I don't know."

"I haven't."

"Thank god for that! Deep down I want to think he still loves me and wouldn't betray me – even if it was you who initiated, which isn't the case, I understand, but ..."

"You're still holding onto him, aren't you?"

"Not tightly. Letting go. The weather was bad tonight but I got out. I went alone to the lecture and didn't feel intimidated. I bumped into you and asked you out for a drink. We told stories, laughed. I described a film I thought I'd forgotten.

Perhaps I'm speaking more freely than I should, Elena, but it feels good. I'm getting back something I thought I lost. I'm saying what's on my mind and not worrying about being denigrated or attacked. Do you know what that's like? Do you know how valuable it is?"

"Wow," Elena said thoughtfully.

"What do you mean, wow?"

"I hadn't known. Any of this."

Rachel considered the veins on the back of her hand, how visible they were.

* * *

Elena walked on a cleared sidewalk between banks of snow and dark storefronts. She knew Josh would be waiting. He hadn't said anything. One senses these things. Between them the unexpected had become the new normal.

Was Josh a narcissist? Maybe she was, too. It couldn't be wrong if two narcissists found each other. In any case, she didn't want the relationship to deepen. It wasn't meant for all time. What was commitment other than a synonym for complications? She remembered the image of snow covering the rotting corpses. Desire, Elena thought, is also like that, transforming the world so that one may dance without fear of where one's feet will land. And if it's only a momentary illusion, so what? The moon is a rock orbiting in a near vacuum but oh! oh! so much more.

She had enough money for a taxi.

He had left the door unlocked. She entered the darkened house and held her breath. The only noise was the occasional sighs of a house in the wind. She padded into the living room, drawn by the large picture window at the far end. She knew

the view and enjoyed the sensation it always gave, the pleasure of vertigo over rooftops and yards spilling down a steep
incline. She put both palms on the glass and leaned forward.
Tonight the view was obscured by blowing snow. Everything
below her was shifting and uncertain. She looked up and high
above the lift of the wind she saw a thin curving blade resplen-
dent against a clear black sky.

His voice came from darkness, "I was hoping you'd come."

She turned, reassured by its familiarity. She located him
sitting in an unlit corner, fully dressed as if at the end of a
working day. "What are you doing in the dark?"

"I fell asleep."

"Couldn't make it up the stairs?"

"I decided to wait for you."

"I thought you would."

"My will brought you here."

"No, it was my decision. I wanted to come."

"Maybe my will shapes your decisions."

"I wouldn't count on it."

"I won't."

"I went to a lecture tonight. On Iraq. Rachel was there."

"Was she with anybody?"

"No."

"She went alone?"

"Yes."

"She went to a lecture on Iraq alone?"

"Yes. Why not?"

"I'm surprised."

"You once told me that she was the love of your life."

"She was."

"We went out for a drink afterwards. She told me you never
loved her."

His voice tightened. "Why did she say that?"

"She said you were incapable of love, that she'd known it for a long time but had worked hard to deceive herself."

"I guess that's one way for her to deal with failure."

"What failure?"

"Our relationship. Her business. It was my salary that kept it alive. Her life in general. She spoke of me with contempt?"

"No. Disappointment. She called you a narcissist."

"She's always had a hard time dealing with successful men. She resents them."

"That's what you think."

"Definitely."

Elena reached her arms out to each side like a scarecrow and began a slow pivot. She stopped when back to her original position, arms still suspended. Slender and uncertain, she pivoted a second time and then again, almost losing her balance, recovering, building to a rapid tempo and then stopping, her breath audible.

"I wish I could read your mind," he said.

"I want music I've never heard before."

He chose an Indian raga.

She synchronized her movements, small at first, with the rhythm of the tabla. The tequila blurred her memory of the lecture, but not enough. It blurred, too, the conversation with Rachel, but not enough. She thought of her daughter asleep in the care of Ghadir. She thought of Ghadir asleep in the care of no one. She thought of Ghadir's son, Mahfouz. His pain and her guilt were choking her. She thought of herself in a pit being buried alive. Get out! Get out!

The tempo of the tabla quickened.

He didn't know why she was dancing. He suspected she didn't know either. He wondered what had brought her to him, this ever-changing silhouette before a window white with windblown snow.

She cried out, short and sharp, as the earth fell away. She shed her clothes without shame, losing their restriction. No longer bound within the definitions of before and after, her skin covered in sweat, she merged with the eternal present.

She cried out a second time, sustaining the note as if forever.

THE THIRD GATE
Piraeus, Athens, Crete, Alexandria
2009

CHAPTER SEVEN

AGGELIKI NEVER DOUBTED the brilliance of her only child. She was convinced Nikos had been born that way. A touch odd, too. She noticed it early, not even two months into his first year; a wandering gaze interrupted by moments of intense focus on anything other than her. She responded by giving little Nikos the quality of consistent attention only a loving parent can sustain. During her daily actions – feeding him from her milk-charged breasts, changing his diaper, cooing to him as they lay in bed or singing him to sleep – she insisted he relate. When he fixed his passing gaze on her for a second or two, she teased him to relate a little longer ... a little longer ... until, to her delight and surprise, he held her gaze and they cooed in unison. Eventually, when the boy hit puberty, she decided he was normal, or at least, normal enough: he related to others, went to school, maintained friendships.

True, he excelled in subjects based on repeating patterns, but she thought that might work to his advantage, which it did. He earned an advanced degree in mathematics from the well-respected University of Piraeus, studying game theory as a tool in economic development. Even though she worked in a bank, Aggeliki never quite understood what the mathematical models her son studied had to do with the economy. Others, however, saw a connection, which is all that mattered.

It concerned her that after graduation his only income was as a part-time tutor to high school students. Why had he worked that hard if that's where it led? Maybe it was the lack of opportunities during a difficult time; half of Greek youth were unemployed. But that meant the other half were employed, and surely many held better jobs than his. There was no point in him being brilliant if he didn't flourish.

She shared her dismay with him. He replied that, as usual, she had approached the issue from the wrong end. As far as he was concerned not only were he and his friends building a new political party to save Greece, they would, at the same time, save Portugal, Italy, and Spain. They were harbingers of a new civilizational force emanating from the Mediterranean, bound neither by the falsehoods of neoliberal thought nor the command economics of Marxism. While their success was not inevitable, it was at the very least possible – so, my God! – why would anyone consider his ambitions modest and the situation humiliating?

Aggeliki retorted, rather drily, that she was not discussing his political hobbies and utopian desires. Anyone in their right mind knew both were a waste of time. She was talking income, this year and next, and whether he believed he would want to be a tutor twenty years from now. He needed to find a position within the system so that the attrition of passing years would carry him forward and up. If he and his friends remained without real jobs, the accumulating weight of those who joined the institutions would permanently crush them. Why couldn't he grasp the obvious?

He replied that finding a comfortable perch – such as calling in loans on families no longer capable of meeting

mortgage payments – wasn't a career path he wished to follow. Given that a significant part of Aggeliki's daily work was
precisely that, his comment cut to the bone. She despaired
of his habitual ungratefulness. She wondered how anyone so
brilliant could make such a mistake. Was he consciously following in his father's footsteps – a talented man who drowned
clinging to an outdated ideology? Nikos asked, drily, if she
truly believed socialist beliefs caused early onset Alzheimer's.
In short, the loving mother and her devoted son continued
their well-established habit of being at loggerheads.

The dynamic worsened when the homeless waif arrived.
Aggeliki found living with Oksanna intolerable. The girl was
a blend of nervous energy and sensual self-assertion for which
the older woman had no patience. Her country of origin was
also a sticking point. Ukraine, as everyone knew, was a failed
state from which all intelligent people fled. This flighty blonde
with her too-evident sexuality was using her emotionally vulnerable son to enjoy the advantages of living in Greece. She
saw nothing else to it.

While the couple was away – she had no idea why anyone
would visit Egypt, let alone twice – she considered a variety
of options to wean her son from the interloper. No workable
solution presented itself. The happy couple returned and a few
days later Oksanna confided to Aggeliki that she was pregnant.

Well. Pregnant.

If that were the case it would be obvious soon enough. Perhaps
the situation needed to be reconsidered. The cries of a newborn
might motivate her son in the ways of the world. He'd be forced
to respond to an entirely new set of responsibilities. The more
she considered, the more she felt her transition from a combative
parent to a supportive, if wary, grandmother might be acceptable.
She wondered, though, where her own life had disappeared.

It was not long before Aggeliki told her siblings in Argos, her friends and colleagues at the bank, the dental hygienist she met in the grocery store, the unknown cashier who served them – that is, it was not long before she told anyone who might listen – that she expected a grandchild. If they offered congratulations she added that the child would be born with A Generous Soul, speaking each word with distinct yet quiet emphasis, as if they were to be forever capitalized but never shouted. No one asked her to define what she meant, but she knew she was referring to a child's innate ability to relate with joy.

* * *

It was undeniable that a malign force prematurely swallowed Nikos' father. A more than competent man who had impressed many with his clear thinking and vigorous speech, in middle age he struggled to remember the correct sequence of three actions. It was undeniable, too, that Nikos' mother brought up their child with a cautious view of the present and ever-renewing fears of the future. Nikos dealt with his ingrained foreboding by nourishing an ideal and private future identity. It was, or so he presumed, the remarkable abilities of this future self which would allow him to evade the tragic destiny his father had lived and his mother imagined. These expectations, ironically, fed his fear of failure and smothered the smaller, practical initiatives he needed to move forward.

Oksanna swept away this impediment at the root. She refused him the space to sputter and stall. Her warm physicality, seeded with humour, dissolved the carapace of self-defeating hesitations. She told him that if he really did want to run for parliament he should do so soon. He knew the issues as well as anyone. Would he know them better in another three years?

She pointed out he had played an honourable role imagining policy alternatives. His friends respected him and would accept him as spokesperson. While he might not win the first time he presented himself, there was a time for everyone and his time was coming. At the very worst – she stressed the word *very* – he would not be humiliated.

He told her he was prepared to fail.

"You should be prepared to succeed."

"Yes, I am. Of course."

It had turned into one of those rare days when the present is radiant and the future unrestricted. As they walked through shadows cast by the temple pillars, Nikos explained the Parthenon had been built to celebrate the Greek victory over the Persians in a war they could not have won without the help of Athena, the virgin goddess. A thousand years later the temple was in ruins but with a church built within it, also dedicated to a virgin, this one called Mary. The great wheel continued to turn – that is how Nikos described it – and a further thousand years later the temple remained in ruins but the church had been rebuilt as a mosque. It was only following the successful uprising of 1832 against the Ottoman Turks that the Greeks regained control of their capital. They then dismantled the mosque, removed evidence of the Church, and began a long conversation on what should remain.

Orthodox Christianity, pervasive and deep, had proven itself successful in rallying the national opposition to the Ottomans. There was no call to revive the previously imagined gods of Greece to play that role. Yet the temple was proof of the civilizational role the Greeks played in the development of the cultural West. So it was decided the renewed ruins would highlight the eternal glories of ancient aspirations with breathtaking architecture on a spectacular location. It followed, Nikos said, that neither he nor his mother had ever known a time when repairs to that architecture weren't ongoing. Every generation offered repairs to previous repairs, and each generation had an opportunity to decide when the perfect ruins would be achieved.

"I like Athens," Oksanna said. "I'm glad I live here."

"We live in Piraeus."

"How many subway stops between them?"

"Seven."

"Seven! Seven whole stops!" she exclaimed, laughing. "Nikos, I want to grow professionally. I want to build relationships with people with whom I can work."

"You haven't been here long. It will take time."

"It won't happen at all if I don't try."

"Try what?"

"To use my skills."

"You'll be a wonderful mother."

"But not only, Nikos. Not only. I want to direct."

"Where? How?"

"All we need to begin is a composer."

"We? Who is 'we'?"

"You and I. We start with a strong composition. When we have that we bring together musicians to perform it and choreographers to hear it. The right choreographer will fall in love with the music and know the right dancers to invite. Dancers travel in groups, so if one good dancer joins others will follow. That's how we find our chorus."

"What chorus?"

"Wake up, Nikos!" She prodded him in the chest. "I'm going to direct *The Oresteia.*"

"No. You don't want to do that. You can't direct *The Oresteia* in Athens."

"Why not?"

"You, from Ukraine …"

"Trained in Odessa …"

"That's what I'm saying …"

"Not a cultural backwater, no matter what you think. The city was founded, in case you never knew or don't remember, as a colony by the Greeks."

"A long time ago."

"Aeschylus was a long time ago. In fact, Odessa was a Greek colony while Aeschylus was alive. Did you know that? The fact I studied there is perfect."

"You're a Slav."

A cry of despair. "Is that so bad? Why does everyone have something against Slavs?"

"I didn't mean that."

"What else could you have meant? Answer me, Nikos. Tell me the truth. If we do the three plays well, will Athenians let themselves enjoy them? Or will they reject them because they were directed by a Slav? Worse, an unknown female Slav."

Nikos took her question seriously. He thought about it. "If it's done well then it won't matter who you are. Athenians are a generous people when they feel honoured. In fact, the surprise of who you are might work to our advantage."

"Good." She noted he had said 'our'.

"But how can we do it well? We have no money to hire anyone. We have no space in which to rehearse, no theatre in which to perform."

"I'm trying to explain that. Pay attention. We can't solve all the problems at once but each solution leads to the next. The right composer will attract the right musicians. The right music will lead to the right choreographer who will have worked with the right dancers and, among them, they'll know the right place to rehearse and perform. That will attract the right actors."

"You amaze me," he said.

"That's good."

"You believe it's possible."

"Of course it's possible. How do you think collaborations work? They start small and grow."

* * *

It was Aggeliki who contacted Dmitri. She remembered him as a thick-set musician and composer, a good friend of her husband's in their early days. She had heard him interviewed on national radio some time ago. His music combined haunting soundscapes generated by the computer overlaid with lyrical compositions for ancient instruments. Encouraged by Oksanna's enthusiasm, she tracked him down through social media and wrote to reintroduce herself.

She told him of hearing the interview and of how impressed she'd been although, of course, she was no expert in these matters. Her son and his partner were looking for a composer for a live performance of *The Oresteia*. It occurred to her he might be the right person. If the project wasn't of interest to him – given his demanding schedule and national reputation – he might know of other composers with the right skills.

She understood he lived on the island of Crete. Did he visit the capital on occasion? She, her son, and his partner were in Piraeus. His partner was expecting! Imagine! A first grandchild! If not too busy, would he be so kind as to visit and discuss the project in person? It would be good to see him again.

Dmitri was delighted to hear from Aggeliki. He remembered her as attractive and practical with an ambitious and somewhat doctrinaire husband. He, quite tragically, had been institutionalized at an early age. Dmitri wrote a brief reply welcoming her message and agreeing to stop in Piraeus the next time he was called to the capital.

Having sent the message, he admitted to himself he hadn't been in Athens for years and didn't anticipate an invitation anytime soon. He began to write again in a burst of honesty to tell the wife of his old friend that he was professionally washed up, creatively empty and happily separated from all his musical pretensions. They were behind him. He considered this confession for a day or two and decided not to send it. If Aggeliki's enterprising son had access to funds, it was wrong to begin negotiations by undermining his own worth.

He had, in the past, written successfully for a range of instruments: strings, brass, percussion, woodwinds, as well as the aulos and the kithara, ancient instruments recently recreated. Very little piano, he had never liked piano. Voice! In truth, he liked his compositions for voice best. Not only were the arrangements unexpected, their emotions held true. But that had been before. A first maturity.

Later he manipulated sounds using the computer, breaking down recordings into various components, rearranging and overlaying them into novel shapes. The initial results had achieved a fugitive and haunting quality, especially when combined with his writing for ancient instruments. Perhaps he had pandered to the nation's musical connoisseurs. They responded enthusiastically to this marriage of different ages, saying he was furthering the tradition of Xenakis and was one of his worthy successors.

He should have fled the country at that moment, set up in New York or Paris. Even Prague or Berlin. In any case, somewhere else. Fool that he was he remained, convincing himself things were improving just as they were, in fact, closing down.

From that moment on, no matter how many textures and transitions he invented, no matter how convoluted or novel the algorithms he devised, he found his own creations boring. His own work meant nothing to him.

Eventually he decided on an honourable exit. He gave up his musical composition to become a recluse in the middle of nowhere. Not quite nowhere – a sun-drenched room in a modest house set above a rocky shore on the southern coast in Sfakia. It was owned by an acquaintance who regarded him as an ageing composer who should be happy to support himself as a conscientious caretaker.

Dmitri, at the beginning of his self-imposed exile, told people a romanticized version of why he was there. It was a story in which water, wind, rocks, sun, the ancient Minoans and the stubborn independence of Cretans all played a role. That he didn't pay rent and received a small stipend for his custodial services went unspoken. That stipend helped him keep body and soul together, although it did nothing to make the loneliness bearable.

Two weeks after receiving Aggeliki's invitation – a minimum delay to avoid appearing needy – he emailed her to say he would arrive by ferry the following Saturday before noon. On the day of travel he regretted having bought a ticket. He hated Athens and Piraeus was worse. His ears would be assaulted by relentless unending construction that never fixed anything, no matter how long the cacophony continued. The streets were filthy. The food was bad. He hated the people because ...

A step too far. He didn't hate the people. The tourists, okay, he disliked them. What he felt for the Athenians was a kind of disdain. How could they support the impoverishment of their country under the rule of German banks while celebrating the empty anguish of European pop music. A dreadful combination!

Not that he was bitter.

He shaved closely and dressed in his most presentable clothes before taking a bus to Chania. He wandered the streets while waiting for the ferry's evening departure. He was again reminded of the large naval base shared with the Americans, the island of Crete having the only Mediterranean port deep enough to bring dockside their aircraft carriers. The island was now a critical node for U.S. power projection in southern Europe and North Africa, as well as Western Asia.

He entered a small souvenir store, hoping to find an appropriate gift for expecting parents. He thought everything in questionable taste and too expensive. He did notice, however, a packaged set of a dozen wood blocks, their price reduced. They were all the same, roughly five centimetres to a side, painted aquamarine, with no further design on them. But not having been properly primed, each block absorbed the colour with its own particular blemishes. They were perfect. The child, no matter how he or she might arrange them, would create a beautiful twelve-tone variation with a minimalist theme.

CHAPTER EIGHT

PERPETUA ENTERED the detention centre feeling positive – uplifted, even – prepared to share her good news with Fadumah's brothers. She thought it auspicious that she recognized the man behind the counter, having dealt with him before. He had a calm demeanour and kind eyes. She greeted him warmly before asking if she might see two boys whom she knew were being held. She provided their full legal names, the approximate date of their detention, as well as pseudonyms they might be using, all of which Fadumah had given her.

He asked what relation she had to them and why she wanted to visit. She replied she represented a society that assisted refugees, and was particularly concerned in this case as the boys were still legally children. She added there was a group in Canada – it was better to say a group than an individual – who wished to sponsor their emigration. A look of surprise passed over the man's face. If now was not a good time to visit, Perpetua said, she could return at a time of his choosing.

He referred to the screen, then found something relevant in a jumble of papers. After putting those aside, he informed her that the brothers were no longer in the building. She asked for their date of release. He didn't have one. She wondered, since they didn't have a date of release, where in the system they might be. He frowned, blinked his kind eyes and said he had no idea.

Perpetua remained standing, holding his gaze, wanting him to take this opportunity to add something … anything. Eventually he shook his head, indicating that no further information would be forthcoming. She thanked him for his time and asked him to call if there was new information, all the while attempting to give him her card. He refused it. He noted it wasn't his job to keep her informed. She could always phone for more information, although both knew the number he offered went to an automated message-taking centre that was rarely, if ever, monitored.

Sitting in the back of a small yellow Lada in the slow traffic of Alexandria, she wondered how best to explain her fears to Fadumah. The girl was no fool. She must be aware that the uprisings emerging from the desert with modern weapons, new trucks, and experienced commanders were well-financed mercenary armies, even though presented as 'faith-based' movements. Fadumah might even have had personal experience with recruiters on the outskirts of Dadaab. Perpetua doubted, however, that the girl would be aware of the scale and reach of the enterprise: tens of thousands of young men recruited in the ruins of once thriving cities, from the restless overflow of the refugee camps or, as she expected in this case, released from detention centres for that specific purpose.

If that had happened, then the brothers were far beyond her reach. They might be on their way to Turkey for military training prior to transit to eastern Syria or western Iraq, perhaps even to Libya. Yes, she thought, Libya, as the western alliance pursued its desired overthrow of Ghaddafi.

She hoped, as young as the boys were, they would recognize the deceit of their elders. She wished them the courage to cut and run at their first opportunity. It would be their best chance of survival.

She paid the cabby, then climbed three floors to her office using the least worn side of the slanted stairs. Her right hand brushed the wall to maintain balance. Entering, she turned on her computer and crossed to the window to push it open. Looking down at the traffic it occurred to her that it wasn't only Fadumah she had to tell, but Victor, too. While it would mean a great deal to the sister, it probably would be received with relief from the stranger.

Perpetua remembered how Fadumah had asked a series of quick questions ending with a direct appeal for the stranger's help. It occurred to her that the girl would make a good volunteer. The opportunity would be life-changing for her. Now she spoke Somali and passable Arabic. If she volunteered for a few years her Arabic would be fluent and she'd add passable English. She'd learn research and computer skills as well as gain work experience in an international office, albeit a very small one. But it was true the majority of funds came from London and the clients were from a wide mix of African and West Asian nationalities. In two years, three at most, Fadumah would be an excellent candidate for university studies abroad. She would not be condemned to scrubbing second-hand appliances for the rest of her life.

Would Victor, who had agreed to sponsor her brothers – an action now no longer possible – be willing to support the sister? It would be a shame if his willingness to help went to waste. On a monthly basis, in Canadian dollars, his contribution needn't be much.

Victor picked up on the second ring. Perpetua explained the new situation. He replied by talking about his F-150. When she told him she didn't understand, he listed the virtues of all-wheel drive, a diesel engine, and a rear axle designed for towing. Perpetua finally realized he was explaining why his truck would sell quickly – being a damn good truck doing nothing in his driveway, deserving better. He would support Fadumah with part of the proceeds.

It was odd to hear him commit because his truck deserved better, but she knew it was a figure of speech and thanked him for his generosity. She was on the verge of asking for a minimum term, perhaps a year, but decided she would do so later. It was better not to push.

Victor asked if she'd be willing to meet someone who worked at the hotel. He thought it would be useful to both of them as they continued to look for Mahfouz. He asked if she'd be open to visiting the Kom el Shoqafa. He'd never been there and apparently it wasn't far. They could take a taxi from the hotel. Perpetua, not wanting to refuse him so soon after his commitment, replied she'd never visited it either and would be happy to do so.

Victor was pleased. He gave her the hotel address, adding that the lift was broken and reception was on the fifth floor. It would be best if they met at street level near the hotel's nondescript plaque. Perpetua expressed surprise at how close that was to her office. He told her it had been chosen for that reason.

After the call she reconsidered Victor's initial visit. His lawyer must have known of the Somali connection to Mahfouz's disappearance, as well as her own involvement with that community. The odds of anyone in her office recognizing Mahfouz had been slim, but far from impossible. The lawyer who sent Victor a distance to personally hang the poster in her office had gambled on a plan that bore fruit. She questioned why she had been so initially dismissive. Now she wanted to meet him. She would ask if he knew where Fadumah's brothers were.

She understood he would not share his information with just anyone who asked. It was the first law of self-preservation: sensitive and hard-to-find information was shared in relations of trust which took time to thicken. Yet … he obviously knew more about her than she did about him. He might be open. It depended on what he wanted to learn from her.

She studied Mahfouz's unchanging photo. Was it possible he was alive? She had no way of knowing. Therefore, yes. Her ignorance created the possibility. Nonetheless, in her estimation, it remained unlikely. The poster had served its function. There was no good reason to leave it hanging. But she'd grown used to having it there. It meant something, though she'd be hard pressed to say what. Maybe the rather surreal sense he was now company for her parents. In any case, she'd live with his image a while longer.

CHAPTER NINE

T HEY ARRIVED AT AN INCONGRUOUS FIELD of scrub grass and stone in a neighborhood of residential buildings. It had a perimeter fence with a shabby kiosk at the opening. A squat building sat ten metres beyond and, further along the winding path, a temporary structure overlaid by corrugated fibreglass.

A guard dressed in green emerged from the squat building, approached the kiosk through the drizzling rain.

"Here comes al-Khidir," Hakim said.

"You know him?" Victor asked.

"No. I was trying to be funny. Al-Khidir is a righteous servant of God. He's usually dressed in green and has mystical abilities."

"So … not him?"

"I doubt it."

Victor paid for three entrances. Correct change was given, but no tickets or receipt. Hakim nodded and they started their way along the path followed by the guard, who turned in at the building.

"The catacombs are beneath us," Hakim said. "They were forgotten for more than fifteen hundred years, which is probably a good thing as they weren't scavenged or destroyed. They were rediscovered at the beginning of the last century. One minute a donkey and its cart were standing in the field and the next minute they weren't. The owner complained to all that the earth had opened up and swallowed his means of survival. What had he done, he cried, to deserve such a fate?"

They entered the structure shielding the entrance, its translucent roof turning the natural light a pale green. In front of them a staircase spiralled around the outside of a wide well, the design similar to the stairs around the elevator shaft at the hotel. Hakim pointed to where supports for pulleys had been placed to assist in the excavation of rock during construction and, later, in the lowering of corpses. These catacombs, he said, were dated to soon after the Roman victory against the Greeks in Egypt.

They began their descent, the green glow on the winding stairs periodically overwhelmed by widely spaced electric lights. Hakim gestured to scratch marks on one of the brightly lit walls, mimed using a hammer and chisel. Once recognized, the marks were everywhere. Victor marvelled at the effort needed to chip away at rock, however soft it might be, to excavate such volumes. He imagined the broken stone gathering in bucket after bucket, each raised a greater height as the depth of the hole increased.

Ninety-nine steps later they landed in a small vestibule with curved benches, all cut directly from stone. Above each bench was the carving of a large seashell. The image was familiar to Victor. He didn't think of the sea, but rather of the branding used to identify a gas company at home. They passed into an underground rotunda and, a bit further, came upon a display case made of wood and glass.

Perpetua stopped to study the incoherence of overlapping yellows, greys, ivories and ochres. She turned to the label, written in Arabic and English. The bones exhibited, dated to the second century AD, were from both humans and horses, representing a small percentage of the total found in that room.

"This is the Hall of Caracalla," Hakim said. "He was the Roman Emperor who wanted Alexandria to greet him as the heir to Alexander the Great, as if he were as important as the man who defeated the known world and founded their city. But when he arrived the people presented a satire in the public square which noted he won the empire by murdering his brother. A humiliated Caracalla responded by ordering a massacre of the young males in the city. The dead bodies were stacked in this room."

"Why are horse bones mixed in?" Victor asked.

"No one knows," Hakim replied.

"Imagine daring to say the truth in public," Perpetua said. "My parents gave me my name because I was born on March 7th, the date of the saint's martyrdom. She and her slave, Felicity, were jailed for their Christianity. Felicity had been arrested pregnant and delivered her baby in shackles. Perpetua's infant son was brought to her periodically to be nursed. Both women were given the option of release if they renounced their faith, but neither did. They were condemned to die in the arena during birthday festivities for Caracalla's brother, the same sibling he later murdered. Perpetua and Felicity were led in before a large and cheering crowd. The wounds they suffered from the teeth and claws of the wild beasts weren't immediately fatal. Both died impaled on the sword of a soldier kind enough to end their agony. It's written that Felicity's breasts ran with milk."

Hakim and Victor were silenced by Perpetua's unexpected words.

"That was in Carthage, in 203 AD," she said.

Hakim switched into Arabic. "You know the period?"

Perpetua answered in Arabic. "I know Perpetua's story, related bits and pieces. I'd like to know more."

"Have you visited these catacombs before?"

"I never found the time."

"But you found time today?"

"Victor invited me. He wanted us to meet. I don't know why."

Victor returned the conversation to English. "I don't understand. Why didn't they renounce their faith, take care of their young, and continue to believe in secret?"

"Her father begged her to do that," Perpetua answered. "On more than one occasion."

"And ..."

"She rejected the idea."

"Why?"

"Read her writings. She recorded the visions she had in the cell."

"I did."

Perpetua didn't believe him. "You did?"

"When I was young. I had read the stories of our martyrs in *The Chronicles of The Hutterite Brethren*. Terrifying stories. They were burnt. Drowned. Had their bodies hacked apart, or pulled apart on the rack. They left children behind, or had their children killed in front of them. I don't understand how they maintained passivity in the face of it. I wanted to know, so I read the writings of the early Christian martyrs."

"If you read their writings you know the answer."

"Their belief in life after death sustained them."

"That's ignorance speaking."

Victor was shocked. Silent.

Hakim returned to Arabic. "You're Christian?"

"Most Kenyans are," she said. "The great majority. Is that a problem?"

"Not at all."

Victor pulled the conversation back into English. "They believed in eternal life. You can't deny that. They drew strength from those beliefs. But they had children here on earth. I don't understand why their desire for eternal life couldn't have waited."

Perpetua laughed, a spontaneous laugh that echoed against the stone walls. She turned away from him, then back.

"You might find this surprising, but life after death is the least interesting part of Christian thought. I don't even think of it as Christian. It was the Egyptians who developed the idea of a god weighing your virtue on a day of judgment. That idea – or faith, ideology, fact, whatever you want to call it – was widely believed at the time. It is still widely believed. But don't judge Perpetua and Felicity by your limitations. I doubt you understand the Christian revolt or the reward it offers. And I doubt that you realize it continues everywhere around you."

Victor was pale and disoriented. Perpetua wondered if it had been wrong to speak to him that way, yet his easy assumptions were insulting. "One either accepts one's moment or runs from it," she said. "Perpetua and Felicity accepted, knowing their choice was necessary to create the world they believed in. That is what you were supposed to learn from your great book, not that martyrs are selfish and seek eternal life, but that a better world is possible through disciplined self-sacrifice."

"But they did believe in the afterlife."

"Not the way you think of it. Perpetua writes of a ladder to climb. It doesn't go up to an exclusive hotel room offering spa services for the dead. It represents a difficult ascent by living one's life through right action. Nothing can destroy the meaning of right action. It lives forever, rooted in love, which is eternal."

* * *

Victor was trapped in the echo of Perpetua's laugh.

He stumbled following Hakim. His legs felt weak, as if about to give way. He was certain of what he knew about Christian martyrs and their beliefs. He had worked at understanding. Yet she had abruptly and thoroughly rejected his knowledge. It sapped him.

They stopped in a room with three low benches. Victor tried to listen to what Hakim was saying, but couldn't focus. Nothing was making sense.

"This is where the families of the deceased gathered to eat on the day of the funeral, as well as on the anniversary each year afterwards. They'd bring the food here. It was bad luck to bring the plates home, so they shattered them in the field above after they were finished. The catacombs get their name from the field, and the field gets its name from the broken pottery. The Kom el-Shoqafa means the mound of shards."

Nothing seemed real, neither what he was hearing nor what he was seeing.

He sensed mourners joining him. He didn't want to look about, but did. He saw faces of all ages on bodies of all shapes. Some he recognized, or almost recognized. Most, like him, were standing silently. Some sat. A few returned his gaze. One was evidently talking to him although he couldn't hear the words. A few, in great anxiety, were twisting their necks and turning their bodies to see everywhere at once. All appeared emptied of individual strength and direction.

Ah! This was a gathering of the bereft. He felt solace in their company. He no longer heard Perpetua's laughter.

Unaware of how much time had passed, he decided to follow his living companions. He entered the dimly lit corridor, walked on wooden planks placed to keep his feet above the pooling water. They, wet and soft, gave way beneath each step, creating small waves and the unexpected music of lapping water.

Empty ledges, carved into the mute rock, ran the entire length of both walls.

Far ahead of him, conferring, Hakim and Perpetua.

* * *

Hakim explained that this corridor was the most recent addition in that underground world. It was designed for Greek and Roman burial. Corpses were wrapped in tight shrouds or, if cremated, their ashes placed in sealed urns. Then either the shrouds or the urns were positioned on the ledges. That simple.

Victor lightly touched Perpetua's shoulder. She turned.

"I'm sorry if I was, I mean … the thing is … the thing is …" He couldn't clarify what he wanted to say.

"It's alright, Victor." she replied quietly. "I can let it go."

"I don't want you to let it go. When I was young I believed in martyrdom. I don't anymore. I think of it as self-glorification."

"Most of the time I agree," she answered. "Young men are hired as mercenaries and told they'll be martyrs. That's probably what happened with Fadumah's brothers. Old men offering money and cheering from the side. But some people, when asked to support injustice, look inside themselves and reply that it's against their nature. They are willing to stake their lives on it. They refuse to be cowed or give in. They develop a different understanding of time and their relationship to it."

"Do you really think that?"

"I do."

Hakim continued on the water-logged planks in the semi-darkness, exiting the narrow corridor into a vestibule bright with light.

Two free-standing statues, not quite life-sized, each in a niche, faced each other. One was a woman, the other a man. Each had a leg forward in the rigid hieratic pose everywhere recognized as Egyptian. Yet the tilt of their heads and facial expressions captured an individual spontaneity completely at odds with the stance. It was comical.

"A transitional moment," Hakim said.

"If exhibited in today's London they'd be celebrated as mash-up," Perpetua said. "Definitely ahead of their time."

Hakim turned to Victor. "Do you recognize anyone?"

"It's true!" Victor suddenly murmured. The male had Nikos' short curls, the female wore Oksanna's tight braids. Their attitudes were also appropriate.

"It's believed they're portraits of the original couple for whom the catacombs were built," Hakim added. "But we'll never really know."

"Are they back in Athens? Have you heard from them?"

"We stay in touch. They're in Athens with Nikos' mother. Oksanna is pregnant. We're all excited."

Victor managed the appropriate enthusiasm. "That's wonderful! Please do congratulate them for me."

"I will. They'll be happy to hear it."

They descended another short set of stairs to find themselves in front of three domed rooms, each with a large stone
sarcophagus. Guarding the entrance was a bas-relief of a thick
snake wearing a double crown. Above that was a shield with the
carved face of a woman, serpents instead of hair. Small figures
– some animal, some human, some a mixture of both – were
painted on the sarcophagi, as well as on the surrounding walls.

"This is the oldest part of the catacomb. The style is Egyptian. Each of the dead has been mummified, placed within a
wooden casket, then fitted inside a sealed stone sarcophagus.
Each sarcophagus has its own room. The crowned snake is the
symbol of Egyptian royal authority, but surprisingly, above it,
Athena's shield with a likeness of Medusa. For some reason
symbols from both Egyptian and Greek traditions were chosen
to protect the dead."

Victor knew the Medusa myth; anyone looking at her
would turn to stone. He couldn't resist staring. He wondered
why she had been such a potent symbol.

There were more floors below, but they were flooded and
inaccessible. They had descended as far as they could.

In silence they retraced their steps: passing the couple with
the lively expressions forever in their niches; along the sod-
den planks, water lapping at their feet; re-entering the visitors'
room with three low benches.

Victor asked if he could sit alone for a few moments.

* * *

He had seen so many symbols, all chosen for their great
significance, all obscure past the point of incomprehension.

He closed his eyes.

He saw a man striding beside a sea of jade under a lavender sky. He looked left and right before quickly crossing a busy street. He turned a corner and came upon a beggar sitting cross-legged in the recessed opening of a closed door. Hesitating briefly, the man bent to give the beggar money. A thin right arm emerged from the bundle of pale green rags, the hand feeling for the smooth paper on the rough sidewalk. When he touched it, the beggar raised his head.

The man recoiled, forced back by the unseeing gaze of a melted face. He pivoted and strode in the direction from which he came.

"Mansour! Mansour!" the beggar cried out. "Why retreat? Blessed are those who meet me twice!"

The man stopped, turned. He approached the beggar and squatted to look him square in the face. "Who are you?"

"I am as you find me."

"Why do you call me Mansour?"

"It's the name given to those who care for the stranger's child."

"What stranger's child have I helped?"

"The brothers who didn't cross the sea."

"I didn't help them. They are mercenaries now."

"Has despair settled in your heart?"

"No."

"Tell me, do you know the sound of death?"

The man said nothing.

"It's a voice singing in the garden at dawn. Do you know the smell of death?"

"I do," the man said. "I held my dying wife in my arms."

"It is the smell of fresh-cut hay lying in a sun-drenched field," the beggar said.

"Singing is the sound of life, not death," the man said. "A harvest is the scent of life, not death."

"Death is visible, too. I see it when the sun paints birds in the western sky."

"Those are the clouds at sunset. You see death everywhere."

"Yes. Yes. I do."

Startled by the last reply, and the voice who spoke it, Victor opened his eyes. A youthful Arden sat on the opposite bench, legs crossed, tears of joy flowing in rivulets down her face.

* * *

Hakim and Perpetua waited at the kiosk. The rain had become a drizzle. The clouds were dispersing. The smell of rancid cooking oil wafted towards them from the surrounding buildings.

"Is it true that your hotel is on the fifth floor and the lift doesn't work?"

"Who told you that?"

"Victor."

"Yes, well …" Hakim laughed. "The manager has a budget that never changes. The lift only gets fixed when he can find someone to do it for the same amount he offered a decade ago."

Perpetua understood. It was often like that. "Why did Victor want us to meet?"

"I suspect he hopes we'll help find his friend, but he didn't say anything."

"I doubt his friend is alive."

This was a new thought to Hakim.

"I haven't really tried to find out," Perpetua said. "I'll do more when next in Cairo."

"I haven't done anything either," Hakim said. "I feel badly about it."

"What *can* you do?"

"That's the problem. I don't know."

"There's a way you can help. A young woman recognized the poster of Mahfouz in my office. I want to take her on as a volunteer but she needs a place to live. It can't just be for her as she takes care of her mother. I'm looking for a room with two single beds at a reasonable rate. It would be recurring for at least a year. Is that possible?"

"If she works as a volunteer how can she pay for it?"

"Victor has agreed to cover the costs from Canada."

"Oh! Then yes, of course. It would be a pleasure. Come by the hotel when you have a moment and I'll show you what's available. We'll work something out."

"When do you expect the lift to be fixed?"

"I hear that question a lot. I always answer soon."

Perpetua smiled. She liked Hakim. They understood each other. "I hope that's true. I doubt if the mother will want to go up and down five flights."

"I'll get it fixed. I promise. And if you know of others looking for a room please don't hesitate. But tell me, how is it you speak Arabic so well?"

"I came to Cairo when I was five." She answered the next question before it was asked. "My parents worked for the Embassy of Kenya."

"We get occasional visitors from Kenya. Not many."

"There was a time when Egypt and Kenya were close. In fact, the first radio station to broadcast in Swahili was in Egypt. Did you know that? Nasser was a strong ally of Kenyatta. They helped each other in their struggles for independence from the British."

Hearing footsteps, they both turned. It was the guard approaching. He wanted to know why the third person wasn't with them. Was he still below?

CHAPTER TEN

T HEY HAD MADE THE INTRODUCTIONS and briefly confirmed the unfortunate fate of Aggeliki's partner. Belated
condolences were given and accepted. Dmitri gave the blocks
as a gift. Oksanna opened the package and smiled. For the
baby, yes, wonderful. She thanked him.

Formalities fulfilled, it was time to discuss the project.

A nervous Aggeliki exited the living room to immediately
re-enter carrying a tray with four glasses of grappa. Dmitri,
wide of girth with a tree trunk for a neck, arms ending in
ham fists with thick fingers, thanked her for the small glass
and lowered himself into an empty chair. He turned to Nikos
and asked if he was familiar with the compositions of Xenakis.

"I'm not. No. Of course, I've heard his music and know
something about him."

"His best music was inspired by Aeschylus." Dmitri turned
to Oksanna. "Did you know that?"

"Did I know what?" she replied.

"That Xenakis' best work was inspired by Aeschylus. *The
Oresteia* in fact."

"No, I didn't."

"I've studied the scores."

"And … ?"

Dmitri shrugged. He turned to Aggeliki, who had taken the chair beside him, and spoke softly. "He wrote music for a production in the United States and then adapted the score into a concert piece. It has three parts, one for each play. When he wrote the adaptation he added new music for Cassandra in the first part and a new piece for Athena near the end. I believe he was trying to tell us something with that, about the importance of prophecy and divinity. There's a very good recording of the whole. Really, they should know about this."

"I'm sure they noted your suggestion and will listen to it," Aggeliki replied.

"A masterpiece. But if anyone thinks I'm going to compose like that they should forget it. One, because he did it already, and two because I'm not him. Three … do I have to have three points? Don't the first two suffice?"

Aggeliki laughed gently.

"To be honest," Dmitri said, speaking yet more softly, "I'm not sure why I'm here. I shouldn't have come. I'm not a composer anymore. I gave it up. I haven't written anything in several years. It became too difficult. I shouldn't be here. I'm sorry."

He looked about the room, now gone entirely quiet, with a rather pathetic and forlorn gaze. He hadn't wanted to say that. He wasn't sure how it had been wrenched out of him. He lowered his head, a big man struggling to be invisible.

"We hope you'll compose again," Nikos said.

"Aggeliki," Dmitri asked, barely audible, "is there any money in this?"

"You have to ask Nikos," she replied, wondering the same.

"This is a professional engagement," Nikos answered firmly. "I'll be frank with you as you have been frank with us, the figure you suggest for your work will be the first number with which I begin the budget. The payment, however, will have to be deferred as the money has yet to appear."

Dmitri sighed.

"If you wish I'll create a corridor in the contract. Ten percent of any and all revenues raised will go to you until your fee is met. I can make that commitment. Profits, at the end of the day, will be shared in an agreed upon formula with all the artists."

"Profits?" Dmitri said, finding his voice. "Are you seriously talking profits when there is no money to hire, rehearse, produce and market?"

The silence that followed began to lengthen.

"Dmitri," Aggeliki said, thinking for her son, "We'll be happy to cover any direct out-of-pocket expenses, like your ferry travel today and things like that. Such expenses must be a nuisance. We can do that throughout the time it takes you to compose."

"That would be a kindness."

"Things are tight?"

"Tight isn't the word."

"And I'm sure, after the major points are agreed, we can make available an amount upon signing. It would only be fair."

Nikos was surprised by his mother but trusted her ability to somehow back up the offer. "Of course," he said. "I should have mentioned that. Out-of-pocket expenses to be covered during composition and a percentage of the total contract due on signing."

"Let's assume I write the music and this project miraculously goes ahead," Dmitri said. "Let's assume we succeed in tempting excellent musicians to play and end up with a good composition well recorded. Who will own the rights to that recording and who will own the underlying rights to the music?"

"Can the income from the recording be shared with the musicians?" Nikos asked.

"It can. It should. Any eventual income from that recording can certainly be shared, with my percentage to be negotiated. What I am suggesting is that you have the rights to the first public production and shared rights to any recording of it. But it would be natural that all underlying rights to the music remain with me."

"Yes," Oksanna said, with the utmost simplicity.

Dmitri looked towards her. Why would he commit several years to a project which, in spite of all his effort and imagination, might never see the light of day? Should it go ahead he would only receive out-of-pocket expenses and a token upfront payment. Much worse, much much worse, he might compose very well and record exciting musical performances only to be harshly judged by the somnambulant people of Athens.

"I don't know why I'm here," he repeated.

"I know why you're here," Oksanna said. "You're not Xenakis and you don't compose like Xenakis but the project interests you. You have something to say musically. Otherwise you wouldn't have come."

Dmitri wasn't sure if he was being chastised or complimented. Yet she was insightful. He did have something to say. If only the Athenians might hear in his work the courage of their past and the needs of their present … if only … if only …

"What interests me, Dmitri," Oksanna said, "are the ideas you had while sitting alone on the ferry."

This, too, was unexpected, but made eminent sense to the big man. He had, of course, considered music he might compose while sitting on the ferry. *The Oresteia* was designed for voice. He had imagined several motifs he believed well supported by the text. They had come upon him and left him trembling. Nonetheless, in front of Oksanna he was momentarily tongue-tied. He managed to answer with a question of his own. "How do you see the chorus?"

"In the first play, as you know, they are older men who lean this way and that, twisting in the wind, uncertain if they should remain in the past or commit to the new. Perhaps they are a bit like you. Resentful, frightened, they look for signs in the sky."

"Resentful and frightened?"

"Yes."

"Looking for signs in the sky?"

"Isn't that what Aeschylus wrote? Aren't they looking for signs in the sky?"

At that moment he decided he couldn't work with her. She was much too self-assured. She knew nothing about him. Nothing! And yet she assumed he was like the chorus in the first play! He was compelled to ask another question. "And Clytemnestra, in your interpretation, who is she?"

"Also as written: a mother whose husband killed their daughter."

"I thought he made a sacrifice to the gods to ensure the winds were favourable."

"The sacrifice happens in front of the troops. It declares the king's desire for their support, which is more important than the love of his wife or the life of his child."

"You don't think Agamemnon is defending the honour of the Greeks?"

"What honour is there in killing a daughter to ensure an unnecessary war?"

"Unnecessary?"

"If a woman runs off with a man from a foreign country, is that a reason for war? Let her sleep with whomever she wants. Send them some wine and wish them well. Find yourself another woman who wishes to be loyal only to you, if that's what you need. Don't you agree?"

"They didn't seem to agree at the time."

"Do we know who thought it a necessary war and who didn't? Perhaps the men did and the women didn't? Or perhaps some men did and some didn't? All we know for sure is that the king wanted the war. Otherwise why murder his own child to get it? And although he said it was in the nation's interest, is he telling the truth? Does he even know his own motivations? That's a question I'm asking you, Dmitri. Does Agamemnon know his own motives?"

"I don't know," he answered slowly. "I suspect they are different from what he tells himself. Certainly they are different from what he tells others."

"It takes ten years for the Greeks to defeat the Trojans but they eventually succeed. They promptly kill the defeated men and enslave the women. Then they celebrate. They choose that moment to celebrate because that is precisely when they have achieved their purpose."

"What are you saying?"

"To kill the other men and take their women."

"They went to war to defend their own women."

"That is the lie they tell themselves."

"Helen was stolen from them."

"Helen was a beautiful woman who married out of her tribe. When Clytemnestra kills Agamemnon it's not simply to revenge her daughter, it is to change the social order."

"You talk as if Clytemnestra is innocent. She kills her husband without mercy."

"Imagine a man who sacrifices his daughter to establish his authority among warriors, then initiates a long war to kill foreign men and enslave their women, whom they claim as private property after their victory. Imagine that, and now tell me Clytemnestra should hesitate, or feel guilt, to overthrow such a state."

"While Agamemnon is away at war she rules the land with her lover."

"Yes, while her murderous husband is away she takes up with another and rules the city with his assistance. Where is the guilt?"

"He isn't of her people."

"Are we back to that? Clytemnestra is guilty for sharing her bed with another not of her tribe?"

"She isn't loyal to her children."

"Not true. They aren't loyal to her. In the second play the son kills his own mother. He re-establishes the patriarchal state she defeated. His return is the counter-revolution. In the third play he is on trial for that murder. The goddess Athena casts the deciding vote. She finds him innocent, arguing the seed of the father forms the child, therefore vengeance for the father justifies the killing of his mother. I question that."

"You question Aeschylus?"

"Of course. Otherwise why do his plays?"

Such arrogance! Yet it was what the good artist did, question deeply and if, at the end of it, one is forced to agree then one agrees. If the disagreement stands, then the disagreement stands. Either way it becomes a well-earned interpretation. To attempt less is to fail before beginning.

"Who are the Furies?" Dmitri asked.

"Aside from being the chorus in the third play?"

"Aside from the obvious."

"I am one of the Furies. Aggeliki is one of the Furies."

"Oh," Dmitri exclaimed softly. "Oh."

Aggeliki stood. She walked into the kitchen to retrieve the bottle of grappa, wondering what the waif meant. Dmitri had responded as if he understood. What had he understood? And if the waif was a Fury was her son's child safe in her womb? Of course. Of course. Just like her son had been safe in her womb. She checked the cupboards to see if there were ingredients for a decent meal, should Dmitri choose to stay. The basics were there. They could make do without anything from the store.

Nikos was talking as his mother re-entered to refresh their glasses. "We need you, Dmitri, to help us build something better than we can do alone."

"Your father would say things like that."

"Was he wrong?" Nikos asked.

"No. He wasn't. Listen, Nikos, I'm sorry to ask this in front of everyone, but at least I'm not hiding it. Tell me, as the son of a man whom I respected and who respected me, do you really think this young woman can lead us in such a large and important project?"

Nikos' answer was swift and unequivocal. "There's no one better!"

Dmitri wondered what could possibly be at the root of such a spontaneous response. Looking for reassurance he turned to Aggeliki. "Is that true?"

She wanted to let loose a torrent of words to let him know of her love cut tragically short for a charismatic husband who had somehow lost his mind, of the feeling of incompleteness that had grown within her, of how she had brought up their strange, brilliant, but very stupid son almost entirely alone and how a sensuous, conniving, impertinent Slav had stolen his heart and was threatening to take him away from her and how she, who did not have much, had just committed her own hard-earned savings to support an idealistic and undefined project which would probably never happen and, in spite of that, the conniving Slav and her ungrateful son would inevitably run away with her grandchild with A Generous Soul and she, much too young to be so old, would continue to close mortgages on the unfortunate and vulnerable until, entirely forgotten and alone, bent over, withered and wizened, wearing a black skirt black jacket black shoes black stockings died in utter darkness and solitude. Instead she bit her tongue and relented.

"She's tough, Dmitri. Tough. Always one step ahead. Believe me. One day you'll wake up happy to realize you're working for her."

Oksanna, hands quiet in her lap, turned her thoughtful gaze on Dmitri.

"Alright," he said, confirming his decision by gently touching the back of Aggeliki's hand. "Alright. I'm in."

THE FOURTH GATE
Montreal
2009

CHAPTER ELEVEN

"IT'S NOT BECAUSE Sameh's coming home," Ghadir said, putting her hands up in the air, palms facing forward. "But …" Her hands lowered to her lap, the sentence unfinished.

"I didn't expect this," Elena murmured. It was because Sameh was coming home.

"Your father arrives tomorrow. Why don't you and Sharon return to Brandon with him? He's the only real family you have and at times like these that's important."

It was brutal but true. Ghadir and Sameh were not family. As partner to her son, Elena had been almost family, possible family. That had been good enough for a time but the time was over. She was being asked to gather Sharon and leave.

Elena stood. She looked about. In this kitchen they had cooked, cried, eaten together, sometimes laughed, rarely fought.

Ghadir pointed with her hand for Elena to sit. "Sameh will have an electronic device locked to his ankle. They tell him he's free to work, that he can go out during the day wearing it, but the restaurant went bankrupt while he was in prison. How is he supposed to start again? And our son …" She stopped, waiting to regain her composure. "Sameh is angry. Hurt. He …" Ghadir couldn't find the right words.

Elena understood, a wounded Sameh needed space and privacy in which to heal. It would be difficult with her and Sharon there. Ghadir didn't think it possible.

"We thought we belonged in Montreal. We thought the laws would protect us. We were wrong. The so-called Security Certificates were put in place to make it legal to imprison Muslims without charge or trial. Don't tell me that's not true. It's what happened. Don't make the mistake we made, Elena. Go to a place where you belong. Sharon will be safer there."

"Back to Brandon?"

"Isn't that where you belong?"

* * *

Elena studied her father as he approached the luggage carousel. He appeared slimmer, tanned, more stern in appearance.

Sharon immediately ran forward and threw her thin arms about his waist. "I missed you. I missed you so much!"

He crouched to return the embrace. "I missed you, too. I did."

"You've lost weight," Elena said, not believing he looked better for it.

Victor stood as if being accused of something. "Didn't eat well. Didn't sleep well. I tried but, you know …"

Elena closed the remaining distance to embrace him. "No, I don't know. I'm glad you're back."

"I wanted to be more successful."

"We know more than before. Josh is waiting outside. He'll drive you to your motel then take Sharon and me back to Ghadir's."

"Did you ask him to do that?"

"He wants to help."

"Do I have a reservation?"

"They are expecting you. Will your credit be good?"

"I sure as hell hope so."

All three lowered their heads and jogged through the rain towards a lengthening line of red taillights. Josh, scanning his rearview mirror, popped the trunk, opened his door and stepped out.

"Thanks for coming to get me," Victor said, swinging his valise up and in.

"Sit in the back with granddad," Elena told Sharon, who quickly obliged.

Josh resettled in the driver's seat. He put the car in gear and turned into the traffic. "It's six hours later in Cairo. A long day for you. You must be tired."

"I'm tired but happy to be back. It's odd, you know, I was thinking about it on the plane. I've spent more time in Cairo and Alexandria than I have in Montreal or Toronto. I never expected that."

"Elena tells me you've booked into some God-forsaken motel on St. Catherine East."

"Is that how she described it?"

"She didn't say God-forsaken."

"Hot water. Clean sheets. Towels. Only one set of stairs to climb." He listed the facts with appreciation. Sharon smiled up at him in the dark. He smiled back. "How are you, little one?"

She shifted closer and then said, quite seriously, "I don't want to move again."

"Who said you have to move again?"

"Mom did."

"We'll discuss it later," Elena said, turning in her seat to face him. "Do you know when you're going back?"

"I am back. If you mean when I'm going to Brandon, the day after tomorrow."

"That soon?"

"I hope my co-workers haven't discovered life is better without me."

Elena considered momentarily, then turned to face front. "Ghadir expects you for dinner tomorrow. She's going to cook something special."

Josh re-entered the conversation as the car slowed towards a light. "Did you get done what you wanted?"

"No. Not really. We know more than we did before, but we don't know where Mahfouz is. I met his uncle in Cairo. He was picked up at the same time they picked up Mahfouz and then, suddenly, without warning, they released him."

"Does he speak English?" Josh asked.

"He knows a few words, but Perpetua, an advocate for prisoners I met in Alexandria, translated. She's been very helpful."

"Why wasn't Mahfouz released at the same time?" Elena asked.

"We don't know."

"Will he be released at some point?"

"That's the hope, that one day the right door opens and there he is, walking free."

"What's the uncle like?"

"Full of regret. He blames himself. I met with him for about an hour. He said the same things over and over. At the end, he told me to think of Mahfouz as a Mahdi."

"What's that?"

"A religious leader who disappears but will return."

"Why did he say that? Mahfouz isn't religious at all."

"He meant it as a way of saying not to give up."

"Why did he think you were giving up?"

"I wasn't."

"But you just said –"

"Did you meet with the Canadian embassy?" Josh asked, speaking over her.

"Twice. Both times they said the same thing. They know nothing and have nothing to add."

"You believe them?"

"I believed the person talking to me. She was sympathetic and made the point of telling me that she, like Mahfouz, was from Montreal. I wondered, though, if she'd been told the whole story."

Josh nodded. "Embassies are good at that, arranging meetings with sympathetic spokespersons who know nothing. At least she didn't confirm the worst."

"Exactly," Victor replied. "All the time I was there no one confirmed the worst."

"They released his uncle without any warning," Elena said. "Just like that?"

"That's what arbitrary justice is like," her father answered. "The decision to detain and the decision to release. You don't know who decides. You don't know why. The process is hidden."

They arrived at a long, rectangular, graceless structure set at the back of a narrow lot. It had identical rows of yellow doors and unlit windows running the entire length of its two stories. Josh parked in front of the unit closest to the street, identified as an office by the blinking red neon sign. The rain had stopped. The black water of the puddles captured the intermittent reflections.

Ouvert Ouvert Ouvert

* * *

Victor eased himself out of the car, trying not to disturb the sleeping Sharon. He lifted his bag from the trunk and led Elena towards the office. He signed in and ran his credit card.

They exited the office, climbed the outside stairs and found the unit. Victor unlocked the deadbolt, opened the door and switched on the lights. Elena picked up his bag, put it on the luggage stand and zipped it open.

"You don't need to do that."

"I don't want you to feel abandoned on your first night back. I want you to think I'm taking care of you."

"You are taking care of me. You met me at the airport. You arranged a lift to the motel. We've made plans for tomorrow. We're in good shape."

"Good." Elena hung up his spare shirts.

"I'm happy to be home," Victor said. "Almost home. And to see you. I'm happy to see you."

"I'm happy to see you, too."

"I feel grateful."

"I'm glad."

"Did you know that the word for ungrateful in Arabic is the same word used for an unbeliever?"

"Is it?"

"*Kafir*. That's what Hakim told me."

"The receptionist guy?"

"An unbeliever is someone who is ungrateful. I find that interesting."

"I guess I'm an unbeliever. I find it hard to be grateful these days."

"When I was young my father didn't want me to be baptized. He was against it. It was a big deal because if I didn't do it by a certain age then I was expected …"

"To leave the colony," Elena said, finishing his sentence. "I know all this."

"Did I ever tell you why he was against it? He said I lacked *gellassenheit*. It's usually translated as serenity but it's not. It's a kind of inner humility that leads to serenity. Did I ever tell you about that?"

"I don't remember." She refolded his second pair of pants and hung it over the back of the chair, as he would do at home.

"Hakim talks about gratitude the same way my father did about *gellassenheit*. It's something they share."

"I'm putting your shaving kit in the bathroom."

"It leads to the right path."

Elena emerged from the washroom. "Dad, why are you talking about a path? There is no path."

Her certainty irked him. "Gratitude is possible, isn't it? And humility? And if consequences follow, that's a path. No?"

"I'm not saying there aren't consequences, but to talk about some kind of path … a narrow way forward to some higher destination, there's no such thing."

"If we're not on a path, Elena, where the hell are we?"

"You need an image?"

"What do you mean?"

"Do you need an image to make sense of things? Alright. I'm not walking down a path towards the light at the end. You might be, I'm not. I'm in a fight I didn't choose. The very idea of forward is impossible because I'm surrounded on all sides. There is no forward. All I do is to defend myself from the darkness closing in. I'm getting smaller and smaller. I've begun to vanish. That's the image you should consider. Your daughter is vanishing right in front of you and you can't see it."

Victor knew what he wanted. "Come home. I can take care of you in Brandon. Please. The three of us."

"There's not enough room."

"What are you saying? There are three bedrooms."

"That's not my point."

"What's your point? You don't have to forget Mahfouz or everything you've lived here. Is that it? Bring your memories with you. There's room, I promise."

This was exactly what Elena didn't want to hear; going to Brandon was to accept Mahfouz as a memory. She tried sarcasm. "Do I start again, this time with gratitude for painful memories?"

He was impervious to tone. "Gratitude keeps one strong over the long haul."

There it was again, the same stubborn hope she had heard at the lecture. '*The long haul …*' How does one prepare for '*the long haul*'? Gratitude? Really?

"I have to go, dad. The cafe opens at six and I need to be there before that. It's what I do. And Sharon and Joshua are waiting in the car."

"When you work so early who gets Sharon off to school?"

"Ghadir. They have a routine. That part of my life works."

"Not the other parts?"

"We'll talk later. I have to go."

"Come home, Elena."

She knew he couldn't help it. It wouldn't be him otherwise. "I'll consider it," she said, giving him a quick hug.

Victor removed his shoes and lay back on the bed. He could shower now or in the morning. He could use as much hot water as he wanted. He could shave, too. He had carried so much tension in his body while abroad.

It felt odd to him, selling his truck to support Fadumah while Elena worked in difficult circumstances. Unnatural. If only Elena and Sharon would come home, then he could take care of everyone. A question of putting in the hours. Overtime. If she felt herself disappearing she must want to come home. There was a school nearby for Sharon. It would all work out.

He should talk to her about Hakim and Nikos, Oksanna and Perpetua. Fadumah. He should tell her that there were people far away who understood and cared, that the search for Mahfouz had just begun.

He wondered if he would tell her about having met Al-Khadir. Twice. And how, during the second encounter, Al-Khadir transformed into Arden. Or perhaps he had met Arden three times, once in the hotel room and then twice as Al-Khadir. No, he definitely couldn't talk about that with Elena. She'd think he was losing it.

Was it wrong, he wondered, to allow himself to appreciate the fragile beauty of myth? Was it wrong to enjoy symbols which promised to overcome change, even though they failed? Don't we deserve to celebrate what we know as if it were eternal? If it provides solace, companionship, a sense of continuity? Was that forfeiting reason? Such arrogance to call ourselves *homo sapiens sapiens*. One *sapiens* was sufficient. We should have called ourselves *homo sapiens mythicus*.

Elena had said there was no path. Perpetua had said nothing could destroy the meaning of right action.

* * *

"I'm sorry if I took too long." Elena's voice was hushed as she entered the car. "Did Sharon sleep the whole time?"

"Yes," Josh said in a half-whisper.

"My head is pounding." She touched his arm. "Thank you for driving us."

He drove slowly, as if waiting for something. Eventually he asked, "How was it with your dad?"

"My father has always been confused. He also thinks each of his confusions is going to be the last, which is why, I suppose, he thinks each one important. I kind of respect that about him."

"Are you going back to Brandon."

"I don't know."

"He wants you to?"

"Yes."

"I understand why you might choose to go, but I want you to know it won't make me happy."

"I don't think your happiness is my priority."

"Would you consider another option?"

"What?" Although she knew what he was going to say.

"Move in with me."

"There are two of us."

"I know that. And you're inseparable. I'm inviting you both to move in."

Elena felt saddened, not by the offer, which she thought genuine if silly, but the assumption she and her daughter were inseparable. They certainly had been. Since conception. But now her daughter was fighting for independence, resenting the existence of her mother, acting as if she preferred Ghadir.

"What are you thinking?" he asked.

"Why should Sharon have to suffer my depression?"

"You're depressed?"

"Perceptive."

Josh considered. "Rachel blamed me for her depression. You're not going to blame me, too, are you?"

"That's another conversation I don't need."

"Right."

"Ghadir is consistent. She's good for Sharon."

"She's not her mother."

"I'm aware of that."

They drove in silence.

"Rachel, or someone very much like Rachel, asked to meet me the other day," Josh said. "She wants me to sell the house and divide the income. I don't want to. The house keeps rising in value. We make as much each year by not selling as we do working. When we cash out none of it is taxable. Why sell?"

"Because she needs the money."

"The person in front of me looked like Rachel, sounded like Rachel, but wasn't her."

"She told me she wanted to have that conversation with you. I'm glad she did."

"You're not listening, are you? How was it possible for another person to look so much like Rachel, to know so much about my personal life, and yet not be her?"

"How can you think like that?"

"I know her better than anybody, don't I? Who she is and who she's not? It was an imposter."

"Just do as she asks."

"Why?"

"She fell apart living with you. Now she's working hard to let you go and pull herself together. I want her to succeed. Give her the money that's hers and leave her alone."

"You haven't moved in and already you're bossing me around."

"Josh, I'm doing everything I can to be conscious in the present, and all that's happening is that I'm getting smaller."

"Don't do that. I like your size. It's a great size."

"I told my father I was about to disappear. I should have added it would be a good thing."

"Don't say that."

"It's what I'm thinking."

"Why? I need you."

"Josh ... get real."

"Does that mean you're moving in?"

CHAPTER TWELVE

THE LECTURER WAS SITTING with a coffee in front of her. She appeared small and less commanding than when at the lectern. An unremarkable woman. Rachel wouldn't have recognized her had they crossed the street together at Jean Talon and Park five minutes earlier. Nor would she have given her a second thought.

"I'm Rachel. Sorry to be late."

The lecturer stood and they somewhat awkwardly shook hands. "Aleema."

"Aleema?"

"Yes."

"I'll get my coffee and be back." Rachel went to the counter and helped herself to a glass of water before ordering a regular drip. She returned to the table with both.

"I've never received an email quite like yours," Aleema said.

"I hope that's a good thing. You said you were open to feedback. Your email address was on the handout, so I thought, why not?"

"Exactly. Why not? And here we are."

"Tell me, do you think you'll ever give that presentation again?"

"If someone asks, but there's no queue forming."

"No pent-up demand for your words of wisdom?"

"Doesn't seem that way."

"How do you feel it went? The rant."

A rant? Was Rachel exaggerating to amuse her? "You were there. Shouldn't you be telling me? How do you feel it went?"

"Okay," Rachel replied. "I can try." She remembered entering a touch late and being surprised by the expectant silence. "There weren't a lot of people but they wanted to hear what you had to say. That was my initial impression. After your opening they didn't stampede for the exits, which is what I wanted to do."

"I appreciate that you stayed."

"It was an effort. I tried to relax, to accept that you weren't my enemy. Eventually I got there. I'm glad you took questions at the end. I liked that. It showed that you were open to hearing other perspectives. I especially liked the girl who asked why you insisted on calling it genocide. She asked what I was thinking."

"I take it you weren't convinced."

"Neither was she. There's something dishonest in how you approach the subject. She wanted to understand and I did too." There was a hesitant pause before Rachel continued. "You know, there's a foundation at the university focused on genocide studies."

"Yes, I'm aware."

"I entered a bit late so maybe I missed it, but did someone from the foundation introduce you? I noticed no one thanked you at the end."

"No one introduced me. A representative from the student group hosting the event was supposed to show up but didn't. I don't know why, perhaps due to the weather. The technician had already done what had to be done with the lights and the microphone so, on the hour, I decided it best to simply stand up and start. It didn't make sense not to speak because one person hadn't arrived."

"Did the people in the foundation know about your lecture? Did they promote it?"

"They knew about it. I asked them for support. I sent a polite request including the main points of my presentation as well as my professional credentials. I asked them to inform any relevant classes and, if they desired, to choose a respondent from the faculty to speak at the end. I made it clear I was open to an exchange of opinions. Eventually I received an email. The first line thanked me for my query. The second informed me that the foundation's programming for the year had been determined and the entire budget committed. The last line expressed best wishes. Three lines."

"Had you asked for money?"

"No."

"I wonder if anyone from the foundation came, just to see."

"I wondered the same thing. I half expected someone to come up at the end to introduce themselves, but no one did."

"You were blown off."

"I guess."

"Why?"

"I don't know, but when I look at their publications I have to say not all genocides interest them. Their major project is capturing the oral memories of the children and grandchildren of Shoah survivors."

"I'm one of those children. My grandmother on the maternal side."

"You said that in your email."

"What are your professional credentials, if I may ask?"

"I have a degree in Sociology from the University of Baghdad and a degree in Law from the University of London."

"You're a lawyer?"

"I don't practice, but I have the degree."

"How do you support yourself?"

"I teach at a CEGEP. *Un chargé cours.*"

"Two degrees and you teach part time at a junior college. It must be disappointing."

"Not at all. I'm alive and employed, neither of which I take for granted. I like my classes. One is introduction to law, a bit generic and I follow the syllabus. The other is the relation of sociology to law. I'm responsible for the content and I'm getting somewhere. I hope to eventually turn my notes into a book."

"A book? If you want a successful career in this country you shouldn't have given the lecture you did."

"Due to the content?"

"It's unacceptable."

"Why?"

"The young girl tried to tell you. It's insulting."

"There are others in Montreal who lecture on recent history in ways that are more … convenient. Having listened to them, I decided I couldn't do the same."

"That might have been foolish."

"I'm comfortable with my choice."

"Do you have a partner? Children?"

"A partner. No children."

"Is he from here, or there?"

"She's from Montreal. We met in England, but decided this would be the better place to live."

"She?"

"I don't have to pretend otherwise, do I?"

"No," Rachel answered quickly. She hesitated, then began again. "To be frank, I'm relieved. I had images of you walking two paces behind a man."

"That says a lot more about your assumptions than my reality."

"Perhaps."

"No perhaps about it. I was married before, to a man. He never asked me to walk two paces behind. He never thought about it, either. Do you have a partner, children?"

Rachel was reluctant to share this personal information, yet Aleema had responded to her queries. "One marriage. It failed a while ago but we separated only recently. Two children. Beautiful children. Both are now studying in the States. Earlier I thought that was the right decision but now I wonder. Is a mother allowed to wish her children closer?"

"Summer is coming."

"I look forward to seeing them. When they come they'll stay with their dad. He lives in the family home where they grew up. My apartment is small."

Aleema understood: a broken relationship, a time of change and stress. But whatever the situation, it was not her business. "Did you go to university?"

"I have a degree from McGill. It was a few centuries ago and I barely remember what I studied. It ended up as a general arts degree. After graduation I started a clothing store and worked with a number of designers. I found it rewarding. I don't mean financially, I mean in terms of my interests. It's on-going, the business, although I wish I had made a better transition to the digital economy. To be frank, I'm not sure how much the design and retail of clothing interests me anymore."

"Why did you call my presentation a rant? I didn't raise my voice. I didn't wave my arms about. I worked hard to remain calm and state things simply."

"That's true. Vocally you were very restrained. Physically, too. Your natural style is drone-like. Yet somehow you manage to drone and rant at the same time."

"When I speak calmly, I'm droning. When I present my ideas clearly, I'm ranting."

"It struck me as a rant, that's all." Rachel drank some of her water. She wanted to get a better grip on the conversation, to steer it in the direction that interested her. "You suggested a few times that the United States isn't a democracy. Is that what you think?"

"That doesn't have a yes or no answer. There's a tradition of democratic ideals that remains strong, especially at the local level. But it's an illusion to think the United States is anything like a democracy at the federal level."

"You're convinced of that?"

"Yes."

"Have you ever heard of Dorothy Kilgallen," Rachel asked.

"No."

"She was a syndicated journalist with a weekly column in New York, also a panelist on the national television show *What's My Line?*. They guessed the bizarre occupations of unknown guests or the identity of mystery celebrities. It was popular for many years."

"What does that have to do with democracy in the States?"

"The show captures the heyday of my parents. I enjoy the episodes for that reason. I don't know, maybe the warmth of a lost world: Groucho Marx, Jimmy Durante, Lucille Ball, Carol Burnett." She paused and started again. "Doris Day, Elizabeth Taylor, Red Skelton, Sammy Davis Junior, Barbara

Streisand, Liberace. They were all invited guests. Everyone seemed to know each other and wished the others well. Perhaps that was an on-screen illusion, but they performed it very well. Watch an episode and you'll see what I mean. You'll also get a sense of Dorothy. The wit. Intelligence. She broke the glass ceiling before it was a term."

Aleema waited.

"At the pinnacle of her career Dorothy suddenly died. She was my age now. The police called it an accidental suicide due to drugs and alcohol. As strange as it may seem, on the night she accidentally killed herself, the manuscript she was working on and all the related research material disappeared from her home. Her assistant died a few days later, also leaving none of the notes and research materials they'd gathered."

"You think they were killed."

"I don't think they would have died if they were researching a fantasy. Whatever they were writing was substantial enough to warrant their murder. Dorothy made it clear to her friends, even in her column, that the Warren Commission was covering up the truth about the Kennedy assassination. It's easy now to disprove the official story – one can go on and on, there are so many obvious contradictions – but at the beginning, back then, everyone trusted the official statements. Not Dorothy."

"I don't know anything about her."

"After her death, it was as if she had never lived. No one in the media wondered in public why she was found in a bed in which she never slept, still with make-up on, dressed in nightclothes she never wore, an open book beside her but her reading glasses out of reach. They didn't ask why the manuscript and research notes had disappeared. Everyone went silent: the television executives, the editor of the newspaper, the publisher who had committed to her book, her fellow panelists. There was one brief exception, a statement at the beginning of the first episode after her death. The host said, 'We agreed with her good husband that the best tribute to Dorothy is to do *What's My Line?* the same way as if she were here.' That was the extent of their concern. Let's all pretend nothing happened."

"Fear does that to people. It closes them down."

Rachel pursed her lips and looked around. She noted the red and black linoleum squares on the floor, the embossed and painted metallic ceiling peeling in the corners, the framed prints for Coca-Cola and Seven-Up at five cents a bottle, the long wooden bar which had, at every third seat, a red and white jukebox. It all came together as an exhausted nostalgia, a past without threat. She felt closer to Aleema in that moment, someone who understood the role of fear.

"Exactly. An overwhelming fear. Dorothy's husband – you know, the good man she loved and who loved her – was at home the whole evening. He insisted he saw nothing, heard nothing. He swore it. Maybe I'm being hard on him. He did have children to protect."

"Do you know if the children were threatened?"

"Like you said after your siblings died, you'd have to be divinely stupid not to get the message. Just because history doesn't leave a copy of threats politely written down doesn't mean they can't be known."

"I agree with that."

"I thought you would."

"It was a long time ago."

"Do you mean it was a long time ago and therefore irrelevant? Or do you mean if it took me this long to figure it out then I must be dense?"

"I didn't mean either. I meant I don't understand why you are bringing it up now."

Rachel was wary. "It's okay if we disagree, Aleema, but I don't want to discover you're a fool. There are too many of those. If you haven't asked and answered the question why Kennedy's death was acceptable to the powers that be, then you haven't seriously considered why the United States and the UK destroyed Iraq."

Aleema's mind began to race. She hadn't realized the direction of Rachel's thoughts when she linked the death of Kilgallen to Kennedy's assassination. But now she saw it. "I've underestimated you, haven't I?"

"Don't patronize me. I wonder if you understand how difficult I find this conversation. Over the past years I've been forced to consider facts I never wanted to know. Now I live with what they call cognitive dissonance. That makes it sound like a low-level headache when it's actually a perpetual nightmare. My generation, people my age, coming as we did after the so-called main events, believed it the easiest thing in the world to know who was right and who was wrong. We thought it self-evident."

* * *

Rachel felt chilled. She blamed it on the rapid cooling of her sweat. A few moments ago she'd been hot and sweating profusely. Now her clothes were damp. She should change, but it was late and she'd be in bed soon enough. She could bring a warm tisane with her. Citrus.

She put the kettle on to boil.

She was unsure how the conversation had gone that afternoon. She hoped she hadn't presented herself as someone with nothing better to do than watch reruns of old television shows while thinking of unsolved murders. God knows there were any number of people like that, but she wasn't one of them. Had she gone too far in her conversation with Aleema, spoken with too much conviction, acted as if she knew with certainty things she only intuited?

Now she felt warm. Too warm. She unbuttoned her cardigan, turned the element off under the kettle. She went to the fridge and took out the bottle of vodka. She went to the cupboard and took out a shot glass. She downed three shots in quick succession. She headed to the bedroom, stripping off along the way.

As a child she had been told that the land of Palestine had been 'a land without people for a people without land'. It had been a phrase everywhere repeated, adamantly so in the circles in which she was raised. Engraved in her young imagination, and in the imagination of her young friends, was an image of a sparsely populated semi-arid desert which, after two thousand years of neglect, blossomed again under the loving care of returning owners. That belief was foundational to their youths. A corollary belief was that those who disputed such images did so out of their hatred of Jews.

The phrase lost its legitimacy at a certain point in her high school years. If there had been no previous people why was the heroic defeat of them such an important part of the story? At the time Rachel didn't acknowledge the *Nakba*, but couldn't help using the word, if only to say it didn't occur. More troublesome, however, was understanding why the struggle to rid the land of these interlopers was on-going. Rumours of ethnic cleansing never abated.

As the laments of Palestinian refugees, both past and present, penetrated her muffled world, a new phrase came to the fore, equally short and memorable: 'The Palestinians never miss an opportunity to miss an opportunity.' While allowing for the existence of an indigenous population, it insisted that any injustice against them was of their own making. Jewish immigrants might have inconvenienced a local population, but they had arrived in great distress and with abundant good faith. They had been willing to build a mutually advantageous state. In fact, the influx of Europeans created opportunities for the backward Palestinians they might not have otherwise enjoyed. For some entirely inexplicable reason, the Palestinians had responded with a reign of terror from which they had neither the strength of character nor quality of leadership to emerge.

Rachel remembered the interminable arguments at both Dawson College and McGill University as a few Arab students, joined by a lesser number of ill-informed self-hating Jews, countered that understanding with alternate facts. Rachel denounced their arguments as rhetorical exaggerations. She presented with conviction the facts she knew, recounting the terrors the Jews had suffered and the unfathomable cruelty of Arab perpetrators. She was confident of having won the public argument, and was warmly congratulated by friends and parents for doing so.

She doubted, however, if the same arguments would win the day now. They would have to exclude a large body of facts which Israeli historians themselves had reported, evidence from Israeli sources which documented the Arab narrative. One could ignore such historians, most did, and for a while she did as well. Yet in spite of an earlier preference to shun facts she didn't like, Rachel came to understand that ethnic cleansing and violence against the indigenous population had been anticipated by Zionism's leaders. The policies had been set early, and followed assiduously.

That didn't, however, lessen her support for the Zionist cause. On the contrary, it led her to the conclusion that the founders of Israel, like the founders of nations everywhere, had been forced to do the difficult things which any national movement requires. She accepted that the Haganah, Lehi and Irgun groups were regular users of violent terror, and acknowledged their importance in the birth of the nation. She also thought it natural for the Zionists to demand sovereignty over the whole of the land, however achieved. Persistence to this end was a virtue, proof of grit and determination. That the great majority of the Israeli people agreed was demonstrated by the number of leaders with known terrorist pasts elected Prime Minister.

Although she had once believed Palestine 'a land without people for people without a land,' and 'the Palestinians never miss an opportunity to miss an opportunity,' she now considered both statements false. The Palestinians had been forced from their land and suffered greatly. Attempts were ongoing to concentrate them in ever smaller spaces and eradicate evidence of their past. She knew, too, that the negotiations in which the Palestinians were engaged were designed, to put it simply, to give Zionist advances the veneer of international legality.

Her sky did not fall with this awareness. Nor did her world dissolve. She believed, rather, that she had achieved a new political maturity. She could acknowledge the Nakba and the displacement of non-Jews without believing Israel could have won independence some other way. That was a naïveté to which she needn't cling. We should admit, she thought, that people use violence to achieve desired ends. Often they succeed. Not always, but often enough.

Those who killed Kennedy had also gotten away with it. As did those who killed Dorothy. Yet the consequences of their crimes and cover-ups left a shape in history that was becoming clearer over time. A series of negative spaces visible from a distance and bound by known information created its own coherence, one difficult to unsee.

Nonetheless, her knowledge was limited. She knew that. It was the reason she went to the lecture, the reason she asked to meet Aleema, and the reason, too, why she wanted to meet her again.

CHAPTER THIRTEEN

GHADIR SAT IN THE LIVING ROOM. The television was on without sound. Elena, having helped a tired Sharon to bed, joined her. "What are you watching?"

"I'm not paying attention."

"Can we talk?"

Ghadir didn't answer. Then, "How did it go with your father? Is he at the motel?"

"I helped him unpack. He agrees with you. He wants us to return to Brandon."

"That's good. I'm glad it's working out."

"Can we talk?"

Ghadir stood, turned off the television, and returned to her seat.

"Do you really want us to leave?" Elena said. Then, quickly, "No, don't answer that. Don't. It's too soon."

"Why too soon?"

"I need to talk first."

They remained in silence.

"When I was young my mother suffered from cancer and died," Elena then said. "It wasn't quick. It was slow."

Ghadir was aware of that, and wondered what point Elena was trying to make by bringing it up now.

"During her last year, maybe longer, I tried to save her life."

Ghadir shifted to hear better.

"I started by paying attention to what she wanted. If she wanted tea, I brought it. If she wanted it in a certain cup, I'd use that cup. I'd ask her questions to find out how I could help. Did she want me to move the pillow? Could I get her a book? Did she want me to turn on the light? I was very serious about it. I believed that if I were good, my virtue would somehow locate the disease and force it to retreat, to leave my mother alone."

"How old were you?"

"Ten. My mother enjoyed my attention, at least at the beginning. I know I liked the illusion of power I had. I clung to that illusion. But the cancer spread and the new treatments exhausted her. I needed a new approach. I decided to convince the universe's most powerful force to get involved. I was timid at first, quietly beseeching God to do what I couldn't. I'd lie in my bed with my eyes closed and pray. I'd stand in the sunlight looking out the kitchen window and pray. Sometimes I prayed with arms outstretched and hands open. Sometimes I prayed with elbows tight to my body and hands clasped. I thought it important to try different positions. When that didn't work, I told my father we had to join hands and pray out loud. We did that every night for about a week. It had no effect on my mother's health. I became angry and blamed my father. He wasn't fervent enough. What mattered was the fervour.

"On a day I remember clearly, my mother was taken into an ambulance and whisked away. I was told she wasn't coming home. The few remaining petals of my faith curled and fell. It sounds like I'm trying to describe a dreadful thing in a pretty way, but it's how I choose to remember that time. I understand now they were taking her into palliative care. I could visit her in the hospital."

Ghadir didn't see where this was leading. But much better the girl talk than angry silence and closing doors. She nodded, wanting her to continue.

"I became angry at everyone. They were all stupid. All of them. I insulted friends, teachers, nurses, my father, especially my useless father. On my last visit to my mother I had nothing to say. Nothing. She held me as best she could. She tried to talk to me. I couldn't open my mouth. I regret that. So much. I hope she understood. I hope she forgave me."

They both heard Sharon's naked feet flapping on the floor. They waited for her to finish in the washroom and return to bed.

"I entered high school the year of my mother's death. I wasn't happy to be there. I expected to be humiliated and I was. You've probably noticed that sometimes I hesitate in the wrong places when I speak, or I fall into awkward silences that go on forever. It was worse in high school. They thought me slow. On the other hand, they decided I was attractive so the overall judgment was 'slow but pretty'. I figured if that's what they decided … well, I could live with it. My real life was at home.

"I read every book my mom left behind. There were a lot. I'm not telling you I understood everything, I'm telling you I read them, or tried. Novels. Biography. Feminism. Historical non-fiction. I was guided into adulthood by the reading choices my mom had made. My dad tells me I developed her habits, starting a new book before the previous half-dozen were finished. They didn't get confused in my mind. They really didn't. I understood each one better because of the others read beside it.

"There was a guy I liked. I thought we liked each other. I wanted the physical intimacy. I did. We were in his parents' car. We were both excited. I wanted to give way. But it ended with me getting pinned. I was saying no, no, no … feeling sick to my stomach. I was afraid of who he'd become. Of who I'd become. I was terrified of becoming pregnant. I spoke to no one and made no decision. That was my choice. To make no decision.

"I tried to prepare for the birth. I went to the classes. I learned how to breathe. But nothing prepared me for what happened. It was beyond me. I was trying to hang on, completely overwhelmed. At one point I had an out of body experience. I was looking down at myself – this poor girl, this suffering creature, who thought she was about to die. She called out. Screamed."

Ghadir remembered the birth of Mahfouz. It was different. It was the same. She, too, had yelled out.

"Then the nurse was beside me," Elena said. "We were looking in each other's eyes and breathing together. I got through it. I didn't die. Sometimes I think of Mahfouz and … I hate thinking of him in pain. I say to him, in my head, 'Don't give up, Mahfouz. Don't give up my love. Leave your body. Float if you can. Float. It will end. We are waiting for you.'"

Ghadir closed her eyes to hold back tears.

"Sharon was delivered with her waters. She arrived like a sprite, riding the river. Labour was difficult, but the actual birth was fast. Then I was holding her in my arms. The first thing I thought was how beautiful she was. I said it out loud, 'You're so beautiful.'

"I hadn't thought I could love someone so completely. And she loved me. It occurred to me, not right away but soon, and the feeling grew as the months passed, that the universe was working in my favour. I divided the people I knew into two groups. There were those who liked my daughter and were happy she was alive. With them I could laugh and talk and plan. All the others were irrelevant. I was happy. I thought of myself as competent and responsible, capable of making good decisions. I'd learned that even the most difficult beginnings can lead to something wonderful. I think about that. I cling to it. I really do. I am clinging to that now.

"When I enrolled Sharon in elementary school I knew it was time to improve my future. I was succeeding as a mother, no one could take that from me, but we were dependent on my dad. I wanted to change that. I wanted to take Sharon, leave Brandon, and study or work in a larger city. She would be attending school from Monday to Friday so I'd have time for my classes, or for a job, or maybe, if I could find a good babysitter, I could do both. My dad wanted me to return to school but not leave Brandon. What was wrong with that university? But when I showed him the official letter from Concordia which granted me entry as a mature student, he took the possibility seriously. He told me he'd moved to a strange city and found his life partner and a profession, so maybe the same would happen to me. He asked why Montreal. Did I have an intuition? He likes intuitions. I told him it was simply a 'pull'. He told me that's what an intuition is and that he admired my courage. He told me he'd miss us terribly but it would be selfish to make a decision based on that. I needed to be free to choose the right partner with whom to settle. I think he finally supported my move as a way to congratulate himself on his own past."

Ghadir smiled to herself. Yes.

"He convinced himself my mother approved. It's funny how he did that, as if he could refer the decision to someone who died a long time ago and then be happy when she agreed."

Ghadir almost laughed.

"Anyway, he remortgaged the house to get the money we needed. He drove us to Winnipeg to see us off. We could have caught the bus in Brandon but he needed a sense of occasion, a memorable send-off. I remember the drive so I guess he succeeded.

"Sharon and I giggled ourselves silly the first few weeks we were in Montreal. It was all so different. We liked it. We liked her new school. We liked Little Burgundy. There were times I felt lonely, but it was a different kind of lonely than I was used to. It wasn't so much lonely as a desire for what was to come next. That's when I met Mahfouz.

"I wanted him to want me. For the second time in my life I gave way. Afterwards I immediately cried and cried. I thought I had made another terrible mistake. But he didn't leave me. He didn't laugh at me. He gave me space, gentle and caring. I don't know why, but he seemed to genuinely like me. He liked Sharon, too. He made her feel good about herself. I admired him for that. Sharon knew his feelings were real before I did. He liked my sense of humour. I discovered his. We talked. Discussed things. We liked holding each other. He surprised me again and again. The three of us began to build a future together. You weren't against that; otherwise I wouldn't be here. We miss him. Even though we're far apart and right now it seems impossible, Sharon and I still want to build a future with him."

Ghadir, in the silence that followed, anticipated a question.

"So where do we belong, Ghadir? In Brandon? Or with Mahfouz?"

"He's not here," she replied softly.

Elena wondered if she had said too much. Or if she should say more. There was more to say. "I want Sharon to stay here.

I want you to take care of her as you do now, as if she is your granddaughter. That is who you are, because of who you are to Mahfouz and who Mahfouz is to her. She has never had any other person in that role. I don't want to separate the two of you. The relationship is good for her. I understand Sameh doesn't want us here when he returns, but that's more about me than about Sharon. If you accept her as your granddaughter he will too. And in time that will make it easier for him to accept me."

Ghadir did not answer quickly. "What will you do? Where will you go? You can't leave Sharon for long."

"I'll return with my father to Brandon and help him settle. I'll give him time to tell me what he needs to tell me. I won't be there long. Two, three weeks. Four at the most. Sharon will continue at school in your care. I will return to Montreal either to rejoin you, because you will have told me it's time to do that, or to find a new place for myself and Sharon. Wherever we go, we're going to build a future where Mahfouz can join us."

THE FIFTH GATE
Crete, Piraeus, Montreal, Alexandria

2009

CHAPTER FOURTEEN

DMITRI UNDERSTOOD the production of *The Oresteia* would evolve through a series of considered steps, each of which needed to be achieved before the following was taken. He liked that, not wanting to rush. He had no desire to cut and paste or adapt from previous compositions, his own or anyone else's. What he wanted was an opportunity to begin again, to question first principles, to compose with patience.

Oksanna frightened him. That was an exaggeration. He didn't know where she was going with her interpretation. That frightened him. In any case, it wasn't wrong to have creative tension among collaborators. She would stand up for what she wanted, and so would he. The over-all meaning of the production would be determined in time. There was no reason to be anxious.

It was only mid-afternoon yet he felt tired. Exhausted. He wanted a nap. He needed a nap. He closed the blinds, lay on his bed, folded the pillow and jammed it under his head.

He heard air blown through the hollow tibia of a deer. The tone modulated in fixed intervals, evidence someone had carved holes for fingering. One such bone-flute had recently been discovered on the Greek mainland, dated to 5,000 BCE. That was relatively young compared to the oldest known whistles, dated to forty thousand years ago. He tried to imagine the earliest experiments placing the holes, their melodic accomplishments.

He was eager to compose for the double aulos: two pipes, each with a reed and fingered simultaneously, one with the left hand, one with the right. Images of the instrument were abundant on classical pottery. He felt confident an aulos had been used in the original production of the trilogy. When supported by circular breathing, a continuous drone from two sources was possible. It was said the goddess Athena invented the instrument after hearing the Gorgons lament the death of their sister, Medusa.

If one double aulos, why not two? The first could be built to copy an existent original in the collection of the Louvre, the second modified according to his own specifications. He knew the range of sounds he expected to hear from each. He needed to find an experienced instrument-maker to achieve them. Finding the right performers for the double aulos might take a while, but there were some. Those he knew would welcome the opportunity to enter a sonic universe full of microtonal dissonance.

Dmitri flipped onto his side. Then to the other side.

He had been comfortable in Aggeliki's presence. She had seemed comfortable in his, maintaining the same frankness he had appreciated in her youth. He had envied her husband, yet that charismatic man with the dark-eyed and capable wife was dead. How petty and short-sighted had been his jealousy.

Would she be insulted if he invited her to Crete? They could laugh about the past and question the present. Or would she immediately assume he wanted something inappropriate? That would be embarrassing. After all, their relationship wasn't yet a relationship. Was it conceivable she would ever desire him?

He adored the visual image of the kithara. He loved the curving frame bracketing the taut strings. It, too, had been played during the trilogy's original presentation. It could achieve a sustained and graceful lyricism when needed, but was also capable of a quick wit. He could use that to challenge the actor's interpretation, to express a different opinion, to show admiration or disdain. He knew the performer he wanted. She was gifted but difficult. That is, she insisted on being paid her value and never left her opinions at home. In the past she had successfully argued against certain of his compositional choices. He should have been grateful, not reluctant, as she had forced his work to evolve. As to her fee, he would happily leave that to Nikos.

Percussion. Seashell against seashell. Wood against wood. Wood against metal. Metal against metal. Gongs. Rattles. Streaming pebbles. Stamping feet. The circular hand drum in various sizes. He needed a natural leader with energy to burn, someone with sufficient stamina to guide a live performance from the first minute to the last, someone capable of tempting the audience with a soft, curious, rhythm only to unexpectedly swoop down from above with the fury of a wounded Chaos.

There were many such percussionists.

Dmitri stared at the shapes the shadows made on his wall. He knew he was on the edge of a critical decision. He had spent too many years mastering the computer as an instrument to abandon his research, yet the quick indifference of the software had led him into myriad dead ends. Did he have sufficient discipline not to be seduced by the ease of application? Electronic recording made exact repetition infinitely possible. Use whichever word you prefer – decay, disintegrate, transform, rejuvenate – the challenge was to braid the indeterminate and random with the narrative intent of the other instruments.

He lived for that!

He sat up on the bed. Would he dare to put a live operator on-stage to capture both the instrumentation and choral voices, giving the option of playback either immediate or delayed, with or without alteration? Dare he be that operator?

A quintet, then: two double auloi, one of ancient design the other with contemporary modifications; a kithara with the irreplaceable gifts of a specific performer; a broad and eclectic range of percussion for a disciplined percussionist; and, if he dared to trust his musical maturity, 'live' computer with himself as operator.

He was very awake. He wondered why he was sitting in the dark at this time of day. He stood to open the blinds.

He'd begin by composing for the chorus using the motifs imagined on the ferry. He'd assume the presence of Xenakis and Aeschylus, each of whom would recognize elements as familiar. He was confident the quintet – now in his mind a tightly-knit group – would achieve nuance and power with the desired musical references and originality.

He would dedicate the composition to Aggeliki. She had reached out and given him this opportunity. He had started again and was enjoying it! Imagine!

What did it mean that she, like Oksanna, was a Fury? Had the two discussed the play and agreed on an interpretation? He should have asked. He knew he needed to meet with Oksanna again, to share his growing enthusiasm for the production and to discuss with her the possible meanings. But first he should share his ideas with Aggeliki. She might visit if he offered to cover the cost at a bed and breakfast. He could use the funds promised by Nikos.

But imagine if he invited her, no matter how circumspectly, and she declined, no matter how gently. Imagine if she saw his loneliness and didn't welcome his feelings towards her. He'd want to hide his thick frame and burning face. It'd be impossible to continue with the project.

He daren't ask.

* * *

Aggeliki walked up the stairs and into the park, happy to leave behind the traffic of the lower streets, appreciative of the sudden quietness. She leisurely made her way to her favourite view overlooking the city.

Today, in this light, it had a hard aspect, unsurprising given the concrete chaos on receding hills of stone. The last time she flew out of Athens, Piraeus had been visible beneath her. Illuminated by the setting sun, the intense clustering of hard-shelled dwellings appeared as luminous barnacles on the hulls of dark, overturned, boats.

She saw the city, too, from an even greater height, from the pinnacle of the European Central Bank in Frankfurt. From this imperial vantage Greece was a spreadsheet and Piraeus a data entry. To understand the landscape one needed to compare sums. If government income was less than expenses, the nation faced ruin. It was therefore necessary – as determined in Frankfurt – for the government to raise taxes, reduce services, and sell its national assets, including the seaports.

Her son fervently argued austerity was not the right solution. He had told her that the economic stagnation which accompanied wealth inequality and concentration of ownership could not be solved by greater wealth inequality and concentration of ownership.

She had agreed.

Alternate policies, he had said, were needed to resolve the budget gap in more rational ways. It would be better to grow the economy through investments that served the population's pressing needs, of which there were many, while raising adequate funds through a more just imposition of taxes.

She wondered how that was going to happen.

Nikos replied that austerity was stupid, ignorant, and a moral failure.

Her response had been withering. Stupid, ignorant and sinful were all words that served the emotional needs of the speaker. They obscured the point, which was to change how the state related to powerful people entirely invested in, and content with, the status quo. Did he have any ideas how to address that?

Nikos, stung, called her a fatalist and stormed away.

A fatalist! From her own son! Ingrate!

Shortly after, he announced he would run for political office. She hadn't said anything but was quietly proud. Her heart went out to him. It moved her that he wanted to build on the aspirations of his father. The waif, too, supported his ambitions. Sometimes it was hard not to like the girl.

Aggeliki believed democracy worth the effort, but had few illusions on the ability of democratic representatives to shape the financial configurations within or among states. Nikos, she knew, predicated his hopes on the moral reasoning of a free and united European people. She doubted whether such unity existed, and if they were free.

Why was Greece treated like a mindless and incapable captive state? A proposed energy pipeline from near-by Russia with its end terminal in Greece had been blocked. It would have greatly improved the country's national income and competitive positioning. Who actually thought it preferable to buy fracked gas shipped across the Atlantic at a much higher price? It struck Aggeliki as both ecologically insane and economically foolish. The decision had no upside, yet it had prevailed.

Greece needed an ally, a genuine partner that welcomed the independence of the nation not just in word but in deed, a partner rich enough to make long term investments on the basis of mutual advantage. It should have surprised no one – although it surprised everyone – that the Karamanlis government had recently negotiated with a major Chinese company to administer the ports of Piraeus. They had promised to commit significant sums to finance needed improvements, envisioning the ports of Piraeus playing a key role in the integration of the Asian and European economies.

Aggeliki again looked over her city. It existed to service the loading and unloading of boats. It had always done so.

She imagined Dmitri on the island of Crete. Like her, he would remember being a child while a military junta ruled the country. As he grew older he, too, learned of the disappearance and torture of members of the opposition. It was not the European elites who had defended or demanded democracy. That had been the role of idealistic youth. It was their organizational energy and commitment which led to and sustained the Third Republic. Would Dmitri think control of the ports in the hands of a Chinese company a betrayal of that youth, a turning away from the ideal of a united Europe? Or might he see it, as she did, as a paradigm-shift towards the renewed independence of their country?

As she made her way home through the streets, small retail stores on either side, she thought of their owners and the workers they hired. It would be good for them if the ports thrived. They might even enter her office with confidence, chatting as if their children had a future in the country in which they were born.

It occurred to her that Nikos and Oksanna never had the apartment to themselves. They would enjoy time alone. It would be good for their relationship. Thinking about it, she should offer them her bedroom. It was a much larger room with better light and soon they'd be three. She'd insist if they hesitated.

She could visit Crete for a weekend, get some time away, talk to Dmitri.

She hoped he'd make time for her.

CHAPTER FIFTEEN

RACHEL ARRIVED EARLY with the hope of quietly gathering her thoughts before the conversation. She was surprised to find the lecturer already sitting at the table.

"You're half an hour early," Rachel said.

Aleema looked up. "You're half an hour late. We agreed on three o'clock."

"Four. I hope you don't mind but I invited a friend to join us. She also attended the lecture and wants very much to meet you. I told her we were meeting at four."

"You might have told your friend we were meeting at four, but you and I had agreed on three."

Was Aleema right? Has she mistakenly given Elena a later hour and then assumed it was correct? "And here I am congratulating myself on being early."

Aleema held up a small notebook. "It's alright. I've been busy. Thoughts pop up and I try to jot them down before they disappear." She waved the notebook towards an empty chair.

Rachel sat. She considered calling Elena to explain the mistake but … really, it was too late to make a difference. Either the girl was on her way or she wasn't.

"Do you know the music of Arvo Pärt?" Aleema asked, tucking the notebook into her canvas bag.

Rachel was surprised by the question. "The Finnish composer?"

"Estonian."

"Why do you ask?"

"I was considering his work. Do you like it?"

"If it's the music I'm remembering, I like it very much. It emerges first as a void. Nothing sudden or dramatic. Slow and a bit haunting. Then vocal harmonies enter, although the void never quite disappears. I don't know how one creates a void using sound, but he does it."

"You're sensitive to music."

"I wish. I took piano lessons as a child and they were a disaster. My parents had hopes but I dashed them. Believe me, any gifts I have don't lie in that direction."

"Then you have a way with words. Maybe that's your gift."

"If so you're the first to notice. I wonder if the music I'm remembering was by Pärt. Maybe Górecki. Is Górecki Finnish?"

"Polish."

"The recording was of a live performance. I know because at the end – a very drawn out and slow ending – there was this moment of silence, then a series of swelling waves, each larger than the last. I was so carried away I even found the applause moving."

Aleema laughed. "My partner introduced me to the music of Pärt, Górecki, Tavener. I find it soothing. It's nice, sometimes, to be soothed."

At that moment Rachel felt a sharp desire to know Aleema better, to ask questions about her personal life. Had she ever felt spiritually married? How did she deal with betrayal? But this would expose her own wounds. She changed the subject.

"Are you making notes for your book? I think you said it was about sociology and law. What's your approach?"

Aleema looked to the ceiling as if the answer might descend from above, then to the floor as if it might emerge from below. Finally, levelling her gaze, she asked, "Are you hoping I'll convince you of the value of my work in twenty-five words or less?"

A relaxed Rachel laughed in turn. "Use as many as you need."

"I don't want to convince you of anything, least of all to like a book I'm struggling to finish. When we last met you suggested there was a direct line between the assassination of President Kennedy and the occupation of Iraq. You also said that genocide in my country was impossible because Iraqis aren't hated, and hatred is necessary for the crime. Those statements interested me. I agree with your first point. There is a direct line. But I want to know how you came to the conclusion. I doubt if we arrived at it the same way. I came to it trying to understand how Israel became a nuclear-armed state in spite of Kennedy's opposition. As to your second point, I disagree. Hatred gives genocide a rhetorical coherence, but you can hate a person or a people without wanting to disappear them. What I've learned is this: those who are ready to erase a people consider their lack of empathy the result of clear thinking. They congratulate themselves on it. They are the first to tell you it has nothing to do with emotions, that what they are doing is simply necessary, like swatting flies or burning hornets' nests."

Rachel was taken aback by what she took to be Aleema's antagonism. She no longer wanted to pursue the conversation. She considered standing up to leave. Instead she asked, "Can't we talk about what you're writing?"

"Legal systems," Aleema replied after a pause. "How they've affected the people of the Tigris and Euphrates. I begin with the Sumerian period, roughly five thousand years ago."

"Must be a big book."

"I'm trying to keep it short. I want it to be useful, not exhaustive. Some of the chapters took on a life of their own but I'm cutting them back."

"You're at the editing stage?"

"Except for the last chapter, yes."

"I've seen examples of Sumerian writing. Very formal. I've forgotten the name for it."

"Cuneiform. The archeologists who first studied it insisted it was decorative, not writing at all. They just couldn't accept the sophistication of what they'd discovered. In the first chapter I look at the earliest law codes, those of Urukagina, Ur-Nammu, and Lipit-Ishtar."

"Not exactly household names."

"No."

"I didn't expect your interests to be so academic."

"They're not academic."

"Law codes no one has heard of from a civilization swallowed by mud?"

"Their buildings were swallowed by mud, not the civilization. It continues."

"You think that?"

"Don't you? They invented writing, the plough, much of our mathematics. Have they disappeared? In chapter two I deal with the Babylonian period. Their most famous laws were those of Hammurabi, discovered carved into a stone two meters tall. That stone, now in the Louvre, was originally found in Iran. There's a preamble at the top which explains the laws were dictated by the god of wisdom. The writing is in Akkadian, a Semitic language, unlike Sumerian, which isn't. The period divides into early, middle and late, and I try to capture the evolution. In general, the later laws are more cruel than the earlier, certainly more cruel than the Sumerian."

"What do you mean, cruel?"

"Punishment is less about fines and more about physical mutilation; laws are more restrictive towards women; collective punishment becomes entirely acceptable. The growing influence of the Amorites is usually blamed for this. I'm certainly not arguing that all the laws in Sumer were positive. A married woman with more than one sexual partner could be stoned to death. There's no evidence of punishment for men doing the same."

"Ask me if I'm surprised."

"If a woman made certain statements, there was a law in place requiring her mouth to be crushed with hot bricks."

"What statements?"

"They're not recorded. If the law was meant to suppress earlier beliefs, which is reasonable, then they might have been related to the lost status of female deities."

Both women sat quietly, each within her own thoughts.

"I wish we knew what they were," Rachel said. "The outlawed statements."

"It wasn't all dismal. There were positive aspects in both Sumerian and Babylonian law. Both held regular debt moratoriums. I don't mean the waiving of debt as an act of pity for the odd individual, but debt relief for all, worthy and unworthy alike. It was necessary to keep a centralized economy functioning."

"Jewish law had that."

"It did. In that respect, Jewish law continued the earlier Sumerian and Babylonian practices. This makes sense, especially when one remembers that Ibrahim began his travels from the Sumerian city of Ur. Debt cancellation is every seven years in the Book of Deuteronomy and every fiftieth year, on the Jubilee, in the Book of Leviticus. The practice seems to have ended with Rabbi Hillel. Some believe it was a major reason for the bitter division between the authorities of the time and the Jesus movement, which insisted on debt relief."

"You believe that?"

"Do I believe a popular movement wanting to keep alive the traditions of debt cancellation was crushed and its leader crucified? It's possible. There's evidence, most explicit in the Lord's Prayer – forgive us our debts – although churches do their best to ignore the obvious."

"Are you Christian?"

"No."

"You might be Christian. There are Christian Iraqis."

"There are. And Aramaic is still a spoken language in Iraq."

"I don't trust Christians when discussing religion."

Aleema raised an eyebrow. "Yet you'll trust a Muslim?"

Rachel smiled. "You seem to know something about Jewish law."

"It's the subject of the third chapter. I introduce the books of Leviticus and Deuteronomy, as well as the repetition of the Ten Commandments in the Torah. I look at certain opinions from the Babylonian Talmud."

"I can't believe you've read the Babylonian Talmud."

"That's where the disputes over Rabbi Hillel are found."

"How can you do it all justice in one chapter?"

"I can't, so I don't try. I attempt, much more simply, to frame the major continuities or discontinuities from prior codes. Unlike the Sumerian and Babylonian traditions, Jewish written law introduces a strict insistence on rituals of purity in all aspects of life, both for individuals and the community. Strict endogamy – marriage within the tribe – is one example."

"Do you believe that's relevant today?"

"For some it means everything, for others it's meaningless, and there's every gradation in between. I think you know that as well as I."

"Yes," Rachel said. "I think I do."

"Chapter four is the Hellenic period. It began with the invasion of Asia by the Macedonian-Greeks, followed by a series of battles against the Parthians. The invaders won all the battles but never the war. They seemed unable to understand why that was, or even how to ask the question. In any case, that's how Greek laws were introduced. Do you want me to continue?"

"I don't know. It's a bit overwhelming."

"It was the research for the next chapter which gave my employers the confidence to hire me. Roman law in the Mesopotamian provinces. I focused on the Justinian Code and within it, the treatise on civil law. That document, the last major treatise written in Latin, remains the basis of various law codes around the world, including here in Quebec."

"My husband is a lawyer. We used to discuss that kind of thing; the Napoleonic Code, how it's rooted in the Justinian Code, how Justinian as emperor tied the State to the Christian Church, how he persecuted Jews."

"He did persecute Jews. He also persecuted Nestorian Christians. One of the reasons Islam was adopted so readily was the persecution for being the wrong kind of Christian. Islam put an end to that."

"Are we there already? Islam?"

"Chapter six. Imam Abū Ḥanīfa, born 120 miles south of Baghdad. In the Sunni world he's considered the founder of legal studies. He initiated a tradition of Qur'anic interpretation which is very rational, very reason-based. During his life he was persecuted both by the Umayyad and Abbasid dynasties, but his ideas finally gained prominence during the Ottoman Empire. He died in prison."

Aleema spoke the last sentence with ironic sadness, very softly: the rational one, the one seeking reason – in spite of great achievements – had, of course, died in prison.

"Go on," Rachel said.

"The Ottoman Empire started small but grew large over six hundred years. By the time it ended it had three separate court systems to serve different religious traditions. Nowadays it's common to hear this incoherence blamed for the empire's failure, but I argue it was this breadth and flexibility which allowed the empire to grow as it did. Besides, it wasn't as if the empire fell apart. It was targeted by European countries who wanted to control its resources, specifically oil. Divisions along ethnic and religious grounds were promoted by the colonial powers. A line of credit to buy weapons was made available to one side, while the other side was tightly sanctioned. That's how it worked then and how it still works now. It was as true in the formation of a large country like Saudi Arabia as it was for a number of smaller nations. We call Kuwait, the United Arab Emirates, Bahrain and Qatar nations, but they're actually spigots of convenience designed to control the flow of oil. All of these new entities – nations or spigots – were set up as monarchies, which brings us to the legal foundations of modern Iraq."

"The last chapter?"

"Next to last. I compare the laws of 1968, implemented after the Iraqi rebellion overthrew the king imposed by the British, with the constitution written by the American occupiers. The changes were focused on privatizing the economy while making foreign ownership of national resources legal. The goals were clear."

"And the final chapter?"

"The conclusion. I'm struggling with it. Sometimes I wonder if I'll finish."

"How can you get this far and not finish?"

"I feel like I'm failing. Or have failed. It's not what I want to tell you, but it's true."

Rachel was sympathetic. "It doesn't have to be perfect."

"When I started I felt I could track the legal interplay between economic forces and gender relations. I wanted to hold onto that, but I didn't."

"I like what you're doing."

"What am I doing?"

Rachel wanted to get her answer right. She thought about it with her head turned away, then spoke from her own experience. "I used to imagine the past as something which got ground smaller and smaller until it turned to dust, as if the past was past, waiting to be swept away by the slightest breeze. But it's not like that, is it? There are events, or we can call them precedents, which become more important as time passes. They loom in the darkness. They shine through the gloom."

Aleema was moved by Rachel's words. "I was thinking about that when you arrived."

"You told me you were thinking about the music of Arvo Pärt."

"I was. He takes old musical ideas and makes them central to his compositions. All of a sudden they're contemporary. Necessary. Even urgent. The writing of law isn't the same as musical composition, but there are similarities."

Rachel was struck by the comparison, drawn to the sensibility of the person who shared it.

* * *

When listening to her lecture Rachel had found Aleema insistently one-sided and anti-American. She had presented sobering facts – granted – but only those which suited her narrative. Among the stapled sheets she passed out at the end she should have left space to list 'facts you wish I hadn't ignored.' Rachel would have written of Saddam's gassing of the Kurds and his shooting of Scud missiles into Israel. She would have explained in an appended note the panic she felt for her mother as the missiles, potentially armed with chemical weapons, landed in Tel Aviv and Haifa. In the end they hadn't carried warheads and did little damage, but did that matter? It was the fact they were launched that was shocking. From that moment on she considered Hussein and his country as problems to be solved. Whatever it took.

She had been impressed by the American strategy. They used sanctions to create a position of strength from which to negotiate. They cornered Hussein, forcing him to trade military programs for economic normalization. Hadn't that proven sanctions were the right choice? As soon as it was clear the regime had no defence the U.S. and U.K. militaries marched in, tossed out his government and hung him. The public may have been deceived about the causes for the war, but did that matter? As for the deaths of hundreds of thousands of children, the fault lay entirely with Hussein. He had created the conditions to which the allies responded. Aleema should acknowledge that.

More, she should take the next step and admit the benefits of American governance. Iraq had been given an opportunity to be reborn as a democracy embraced by the West. It could join the global community and receive loans from the World Bank and the IMF. Its prosperity would soar. The histories of Japan and Germany were proof. Each had been crushed in a terrible war yet sixty years later both were advanced economic powerhouses. The leaders of the Middle East needed to learn from history. That was the problem … they never did.

There was a time when such thoughts would have soothed Rachel's doubts. Yet beneath a mottled sky on this first day of spring, in the corner of a small café filled with tired and dusty nostalgia, at a small table opposite an informed and thoughtful émigré, they didn't offer their usual assurance. Was she really so indifferent to the experience of the Iraqi people as to believe the violence orchestrated against them was a moment of liberation? Should she be honest and admit she had never wanted Iraq liberated – whatever that was supposed to mean – had, in fact, wanted Hussein dead, the military destroyed and the country greatly weakened? She believed the sequence of sanctions, invasion and occupation met all three objectives. She could add, too, that the best way to permanently achieve them was to give the Kurds the north while helping the Shia and Sunni to kill each other over whatever remained.

Aleema wouldn't be surprised by these thoughts. No, not at all. She had said Iraq's suffering wouldn't be limited to this generation or the next. She knew what the country faced.

What concerned Rachel was that the Middle Eastern Wars – that is how she now collectively understood them – never came to an end. Palestine and its allies had been crushed numerous times in major actions in 48, 56, 67 and 73. The militants who fled the country were defeated again in Lebanon in 82. Popular uprisings were brutally suppressed during the whole of that time, the latest being Cast Lead. Yet the conflict continued. Not only were the wars interminable, the alliances within the resistance deepened. The poor of southern Lebanon hadn't been defeated during Israeli occupation, they had rallied to support Hezbollah, a popular militia now more effective than Lebanon's national army.

Tel Aviv and Washington both claimed Iran coordinated this resistance. If that were true, Rachel thought, Iran needed to be destroyed sooner rather than later. It could be attacked from the air. Should the regime respond with a real counter-attack, not Hussein's token missiles, the United States would totally destroy Israel's enemy. Rachel had no doubt of it. America would move swiftly, if only to deter Israel from using its undeclared nuclear arsenal.

Yet post-revolutionary Iran was not Hussein's Iraq. The population under Khomenei had shed any illusions about the goodwill of Western society and the superiority of its institutions. They had dug in to rely on their own resources and cultural traditions. When looking abroad for support they did so to the East. Rachel grasped that no matter the millions killed, or the eradication of military and domestic infrastructure, Iranian resistance would continue to evolve.

What had Aleema said about the invading Greeks? They couldn't understand why they won all the battles but lost the war, and were incapable of even asking the question.

* * *

"Do you write about Khomeini?" Rachel asked. "The Iranian revolution?"

"No," Aleema replied. "It's too early to judge Khomeini as a legislator."

"You call the tyrant a legislator?"

"Someone who writes laws, not necessarily someone you agree with. His reputation is dependent on the long-term evaluation of his reforms. His role has been to merge Islamic jurisprudence with Iranian democracy."

"You support the Iranian revolution?"

"It's complicated."

"No, it's simple. You're a woman. You're sane. You have the concerns of a humanist. You can't support the mullahs."

"You can't imagine a humanist core to the Iranian revolution, can you?"

"No."

"That's too bad. You can't see the humanist core within Islam either, can you?"

"I don't know enough about it," Rachel said, deflecting from her genuine feelings.

"When young I abhorred Khomeini and everything about him. To us he was the wrong road taken."

"Of course," Rachel said with obvious relief.

"After the revolution our countries fought a long and bitter war. You're aware of that."

Rachel nodded agreement. She knew there had been a war, but not what it was like, nor how long it had lasted.

"We saw it as a contest between the Iranian revolution led by Khomeini – religious, doctrinaire, regressive – and the Ba'ath Party led by Hussein – nationalist, socialist, modern. At the time the entire West championed Hussein. They sold him weapons, as many as possible, including chemical weapons. No one objected to selling chemical weapons to Iraq as long as they were to be used against Iranians. No one at all. To our everlasting shame we did use them, then again, near the end of the war, against Kurdish nationalists. None of us knew at the time, and only learned later, that the US was also selling weapons to Iran. Imagine. The real policy of the beautiful West – and by that I mean what actually happened – was to sell arms to both sides in the hope we'd fight each other to exhaustion. Which we did. A decade of sorrow."

Rachel wondered where this was going.

"When the Anglo-Americans occupied us, the first thing they did, with great thoroughness, was to destroy the Ba'ath party. Anyone who had been a member couldn't have a role in the new government. All military leaders and personnel were fired, establishing the perfect conditions for a civil war. Do you think that was a mistake, the civil war that followed, or was it intentional? In any case the government we'd supported no longer existed and Iran, the country we abhorred as the wrong road taken, was now the only sovereign government standing in the region."

Rachel understood where this was going. "I'm not sure it will be standing for long."

Aleema paused. "Do you know something I don't?"

"You want the resistance in Iraq to align with Iran, don't you? But that will delay the departure of US troops. It even threatens their leaving."

"Rachel, the American military only leaves when forced. They are still in Japan, South Korea, Germany. They're not in Vietnam, which proves my point. I want to keep Iraq whole and end the occupation. Why shouldn't I align with my neighbour fighting the same enemy? Islam's initial struggle was to overcome the tribalism that weakened us. We can use our common faith to do it again, to heal our wounds and move forward. We're not barbarian tribes waiting to be forced into ever smaller cages."

"What are you talking about?"

"The Yinon plan."

"You don't believe that, do you?"

"An American general confirmed there were seven Muslim nations to defeat. He listed them: Iraq, Syria, Lebanon, Libya, Somalia, Sudan, ending with the largest, Iran. The intent is to divide each of us along ethnic lines."

"I know it's rumoured, yes, but …"

"The plan was formalized in the Israeli government report 'A Clean Break', then repeated in the American policy paper 'A Project for A New American Century'. That paper clearly stated the need for a catastrophic and catalyzing event – how did they put it, 'like a new Pearl Harbor' – to get public support for the coming wars. After 9/11 neoconservatives implemented the plan with the invasion of Iraq. What's breathtaking is that Western media claim what I just said is a conspiracy, despite a sequence of intentions clearly written down and endorsed by people in power."

"You didn't mention any of this in your lecture."

"Everything in my lecture I can prove. I can't prove the Americans and the British are committed to implementing the Oded Yinon plan. If I'm right the proof will come."

"The proof won't come."

"There's a civil war in Iraq now."

"Between Kurds, Sunni and Shia, people who hate each other so much they refuse to live together."

"Baghdad was not a divided city before the occupation. There were no checkpoints, no cement barricades. We intermarried and brought up each other's children. But now extremist elements receive foreign funding to tear the country apart. We will beat them, Rachel, and we will, eventually, force the occupiers out. Then we'll have that deep momentum rooted in the shared experience of a successful resistance, as in Iran."

"I see why you're having trouble with the last chapter," Rachel said. "You go on and on as if law and reason are joined at the hip, that by studying them we'll learn how to move forward, then you throw it all away … and for what? An alliance with a well-armed religious movement."

"An alliance with a government willing to protect its people."

Rachel was taken aback by these words, not because her analysis differed from Aleema's, but because it was the same. That was exactly the reason she supported Israel.

It was at that moment Elena entered the café, vulnerable and unsure of herself. She carried the few remaining posters which her father hadn't distributed. While she understood it was ridiculously naïve on her part – what could someone from Iraq, however well-informed, possibly do about a person held in an Egyptian prison – she nonetheless had decided to give one to the lecturer.

CHAPTER SIXTEEN

PACING BACK AND FORTH between the two bedrooms as if trying to remember something mislaid, Oksanna found herself oddly moved. She hadn't expected such consideration.

Not that long ago Aggeliki had shared the larger room with her husband. On its walls had been many traces of their marriage. Now they were gone. The older woman had gathered her cherished mementos, emptied the drawers and closets, and asked Nikos and Oksanna to move in during her absence. When she returned she would take their smaller room.

Coming to rest in the doorway, Oksanna imagined Aggeliki lying beside her husband as they quietly discussed his increasing forgetfulness. Did they choose not to use the word dementia, hoping to avoid the finality of it? Or had they laughed about his eventual consolation: the memory of missing memories would also be forgotten.

Oksanna retreated to the kitchen and sat. Using both hands she cradled the underside of her swelling womb. Nikos' father had lived with the increasing illusiveness of his past, the very inverse of what Cassandra had suffered, hers being the certainty of her future.

She began life as a Trojan princess, a life innocent of foresight. Unfortunately the god Apollo desired the youthful rush of her beauty. She rejected his advances, which inflamed his passion. He offered her knowledge of the future in exchange for her favours.

Cassandra had agreed and her visions began. Unsequenced intuitions arose, merged into probabilities. These thickened and coalesced into brutal certainty. Cassandra saw her Apollo, the divine Apollo, he to whom she was now promised, assist the Greeks to massacre the Trojan men and enslave the women.

Horrified, Cassandra again rejected his advances.

A furious Apollo, unable to rescind powers willfully given, chose to alter their consequence. She might know the future but none of her prophecies would be believed. Not one. Try as she might, those Cassandra needed to warn would consider her a liar and a fool.

The destruction happened as she foresaw. A wooden horse was pulled through the city gates. The Greek soldiers poured from its belly at night. The Trojan men were slaughtered. The women enslaved.

Victorious, the foreign troops chose her, the prettiest of ornaments, as a gift for their king. Agamemnon received her as his right. Upon return to his native city he paraded her in his chariot. She stood there beside him, the beautiful remnant of a defeated people. As all knew, any child she birthed would be of his tribe, not hers.

Cassandra listened in silence as Clytemnestra welcomed the king with a fabric of lies. She watched in silence as the village women lay rich carpets between the chariot and the castle door. She remained unmoved and unmoving as Agamemnon strode barefoot along the red-purple path, his queen following. She watched in stillness as they entered the castle.

Clytemnestra re-emerged and called for the slave to join them. The time of sacrifice was now. Cassandra didn't move. The queen, with a gesture of impatience, turned and re-entered.

Only after the queen entered the castle door a second time did Cassandra release her grief. She cried the name Apollo, which soared as a disfiguring howl. The wail shattered into short phrases, sharing her rough pain.

The chorus, bewildered to learn she knew their language, listened as she recounted the crimes of their city: infanticide, parricide, rape, the feeding of slaughtered children to parents.

A call and response began.

Cassandra shifted the narrative from what had been to what would be. The agitated chorus acknowledged the intoxications of their past but denied their evident future.

Cassandra understood. Of course. Her visions would not be believed. Not one. Not in Troy. Not here.

She stepped down from the chariot and calmly entered the castle. She was killed by the same knife used to slay the king.

* * *

Oksanna stood and went to the sink. She filled a glass of water and drank. It was cool and refreshing. She hadn't realized how thirsty she was.

She walked again through the apartment and felt the presence of the young Aggeliki. She imagined how she had rejoiced in her marriage, with the birth of her child.

On the night Oksanna first met Nikos she had explained that many could see the future. Many. He replied it was impossible. While we can remember the past and see the present, we only imagine the future. Anything else, he insisted, is absurd.

How odd, she had thought. Was he really that simple? Did he truly believe we use our present to evaluate our past and on that foundation build a future? It doesn't work like that. It can't work like that. The future is always with us, appearing as an intention powerful enough to shape all the thoughts that follow.

Nikos said he didn't understand.

She replied it was everywhere visible.

He told her she had lost him.

She told him she would share three visions of her death. In the first she was running up the stairs in a large building, then along a wide corridor looking for a place to hide. Unknown persons struck her from behind. They tore off her clothes from the waist down and raped her. They drenched her face and upper body with gas and lit it. That was in Odessa, where she had studied and worked. In the second vision, in her hometown of Sloviansk, she and her young son were lying on the ground outside a bus shelter. Her legs had been blown off by a mortar. Her head was turned towards her young son lying motionless just beyond her reach. He wore his best blue jacket. Glass shards covered them. Her third vision was in Mariupol ...

He stopped her. Don't go on. Don't do this. You are inventing terrible images. Neurons firing in your brain. Nothing more.

She replied that fear clarified the intentions she saw. She was simply telling him what she knew.

He reminded her – as if she needed to be reminded – that she didn't have a child. None of what she saw could possibly be true. She asked him if she would always be without child.

He confessed, later, that her visions were a burden. They wouldn't leave him. If she lived in Piraeus they couldn't happen. She should return with him. He loved her.

Oksanna sat in a long silence. She rose to rinse her empty glass and place it on the drying rack. She went to the smaller bedroom and gathered their belongings to transfer to their new room.

CHAPTER SEVENTEEN

Hᴀᴋɪᴍ ᴛᴏʟᴅ Yᴀssᴇʀ that the couch where he rested between jobs was to be replaced by small tables and chairs.
Although surprised by this unwelcome news, Yasser replied he
would make other arrangements and stated his appreciation
for Hakim's past kindness.

Hakim clarified he wasn't trying to get rid of Yasser, on
the contrary, he was asking him to play a more active role.
Given his proven ability to arrive early every morning, and his
experience in kitchens, would he accept the responsibility of
organizing and running a new breakfast option for the hotel's
guests? It would mean preparing for, and being present at,
the buffet from seven until noon, six mornings out of seven,
Fridays off, for a thirty-hour week. If it interested him, could
he have it up and running by … like, yesterday?

"What's happening?" Yasser asked. "What has changed?"

Hakim explained. The previous long-time manager fell ill
and the owner didn't expect him to return. The owner had,
therefore, promoted Hakim from Reception to Assistant
Manager, asking him to assume extra responsibilities. When
queried who would replace the Manager the owner indicated
the position was to remain vacant, at least for a while. Hakim

immediately grasped he was being given a chance to prove himself. Having recently secured a recurring monthly rental for one of the larger rooms, he asked for, and received, permission to use that money for certain improvements, including the service elevator and a breakfast nook.

Yasser was impressed. Hakim was destined for greater things. Working with him might be the opportunity he needed. After military service Yasser had accepted a two-year contract as a security guard in the United Arab Emirates. He returned to Alexandria with some savings and a desire to find a life partner, but it hadn't worked out. He worked too much. It would be better to work a job and a half rather than two. At the very least he wouldn't need to cross the city every morning. If the breakfast option proved successful he'd have his foot in the door reporting to someone he liked. Pay was not the most important consideration. He was looking for a position built on reciprocal commitments. In a word, loyalty. If there was to be movement up a ladder he wanted to be in line, not overlooked for someone's cousin or nephew.

Hakim asked Yasser to organize promotional photographs for the hotel's website. They should show at a glance that the buffet didn't serve instant coffee with artificial whitener, but brewed coffee in a comfortable setting, along with fresh fruit and baked goods.

Yasser removed the printed advertisements and posters stuck to the walls and painted the alcove a fresh mid-tone blue. That there was a link between a fading poster and his new employment didn't occur to him. He arranged a stack of white plates on a light grey service table in front of the blue wall; added a large glass bowl with freshly cut fruit, as well as a yellow ceramic bowl filled with boiled eggs; filled a transparent pitcher with orange juice and tossed a half dozen uncut oranges around its base; filled a platter with buttered toast neatly cut down the middle and an even larger platter with freshly baked croissants. Finally, he added a pot of steaming coffee in a French press.

He took a sequence of photos from different angles and then chose a few to upload. The results were attractive and convincing.

* * *

Fadumah's mother spent most of each day lying quietly on her side, her head turned towards the two tall windows framing the azure intensity of an ever-present sky. The neighbouring buildings were not tall enough to cast a shadow and she enjoyed light from dawn to dusk. The sounds of the city rose from the streets below, sufficiently clear to denote the rhythms of the day, sufficiently muted to avoid being oppressive. If she wanted darkness or silence, she could ask her daughter to close the shutters, which she had done only once.

She didn't know how Fadumah accomplished it, but her daughter had found them living arrangements in Alexandria far exceeding her expectations. The room was easily large enough for two single beds, each of which had a freshly painted white cane chair beside it. The closet was much larger than they would ever need. There was never a shortage of running water in the attached washroom, either hot or cold. Bedsheets were changed every third day, arriving crisp and ironed. And there were no stairs to be climbed, as their floor was serviced by a working elevator.

Although she hadn't discussed the decision with her daughter, she believed it was understood. She would allow herself to suck on ice – it was soothing – but she would not eat. Eating gave her more pain than comfort. She didn't know the physical cause, something deep in her chest, but accepted the condition as fatal.

She remembered the last time she held her youngest child. Like cradling a bird. No, like holding a feather. Her death, and the knowledge their enemies were soon to be headquartered in Baidoa, had caused Omar and her to flee the country with their remaining children. They moved from Baidoa to Dadaab, from Dadaab to Cairo, and now, most recently, she and Fadumah had relocated to Alexandria. Another destination loomed. She prayed that the errors of her ways be met with mercy and compassion. She asked to awake among the honoured.

She could never imagine one of her sons without the other. Whether playing or fighting they had been inseparable, a blur of motion, rambunctious and happy. She remembered them boarding the vessel bound for Italy, which never arrived. She asked daily for Fadumah to press the Kenyan for information on where they were, but the woman never knew more than the day before. The mother didn't expect to see her sons again. She prayed they would grasp how important it was to stay together, to take care of each other, now that it truly mattered.

Omar had died in a hail of bullets on a hot and muggy day. It was unclear to her why he'd been killed. That he sided with the Union of Islamic Courts was consistent with their upbringing. She considered it evidence of his virtue, not criminality. Their self-chosen exile to Egypt was meant to be a new beginning, away from the earlier struggles. They had called Cairo the City of Hope. She now called it the City of Unexplained Tragedy.

She was grateful that, when it came, Omar's death had been quick. *The eyes shed tears and the heart is grieved, but we will not say anything except that which pleases our Lord.*

She prayed Omar and her youngest would be waiting for her. She knew of no reason to question that reality. In a hospital they would name her ailment and give drugs to delay the inevitable. That was what she didn't want. She wanted to arrive at her point of departure sooner, not later. Of course there would be pain. She'd be tested during the final weeks, yet was confident she could endure it. Her example was important for Fadumah, who would witness and remember.

Her eldest child was drifting from Islam; nonetheless, beginning that evening, she'd agreed to read out loud from Sura Ya-Sin.

They still needed to discuss the cleansing of her body, where to obtain red adar, how to fasten the strips of cloth to hold her limbs in place, and the reciting of final prayers. She overheard Fadumah ask Hakim if, when the moment arrived, she could use one of the hotel sheets as a shroud. He quickly agreed. Knowing the burial needed to happen soon after death, he also offered to help find a suitable plot.

God is merciful.

* * *

Hakim chose the three photographs to hang in the breakfast alcove. Two in panorama format were placed one above the other, each in a black metal frame. The lower was of the empty ruins of Alexandria's Roman amphitheatre beneath a turbulent, cloud-filled, sky. The higher captured contemporary pedestrians enjoying Le Corniche on a clear and beautiful day. They were both in full colour with saturated hues and dark shadows, drawing the viewer towards them and holding their interest. The third photo, in portrait format and an ornate wooden frame, was placed to their right. The image was of a sculpture of a woman in tight braids gazing from the darkness. Though the body was carved out of scale and awkwardly posed, the strong impression was a portrait of someone intelligent and lively. Yasser was disoriented by the image, even more so after Hakim told him the woman was pregnant with his child. Yasser decided this was a mystery he didn't need to understand.

"I should have asked this earlier, Yasser, but it slipped my mind. Have you ever been charged with a crime?"

"No."

"Spent time in prison?"

"No. Never." He took a deep breath. "My eldest brother has."

"You didn't have to tell me that. I asked about you, not your brother."

"I know, but I don't want you to use him against me later."

"I wouldn't do that," Hakim replied.

Yasser didn't know if that was true. "Better you know now. He's a salafi who looks the part. It attracts attention."

"You don't share his views?"

"I don't know his views."

Hakim suspected Yasser's reply, but his intent was clear. No reason to worry.

Yasser used the better part of a day to reorganize and clean the storage room. He threw out the older brooms and mops as well as a chaos of empty containers. He rearranged what remained and found a more efficient way to shelve the liquid detergents. The frame of the window at the back had been painted shut. He scraped it sufficiently to make it functional again. He washed down the walls and mopped the floor. The smell of the cleansing liquids was strong, but otherwise the results were ideal. His room had a door that closed and a window that opened, as well as sufficient floor space to lay a narrow roll-up mattress.

* * *

Her clenched fists opened during the last exhalation. Her gnarled fingers separated. The chest subsided. The jaw relented.

Fadumah placed an arm behind the limp shoulders and held her cheek against her mother's forehead. She cried freely. Finally she let go and returned to the white wicker chair. She remained still and quiet, believing the mother present. Hovering.

Eventually there was a shift, perhaps a dimming of light, perhaps a fall in the temperature.

Fadumah removed the sheet and undressed the body for the final cleansing. She spoke as she washed, telling her mother she was strong, beautiful, and would certainly wake among the honoured.

The final prayers took place the same evening. Fadumah, Perpetua, Hakim and Yasser gathered around the single bed. The body, shrouded, small, monumental, lay on fresh sheets. A merciful breeze came through the open windows. Hakim read excerpts from the sixth sura of the sacred book. He also read a prayer given to him by Fadumah, and another he had kept from his father's ceremony. Not being religious he was uncertain how he had ended up with this honorary function, but saw no reason to shirk it. He spoke the words of comfort with a relaxed intimacy. Fadumah also spoke. Having first explained how important it was to get her words right, she continued mostly in her mother's tongue. Perpetua asked if she could sing a song which welcomed death as a joyous event. It would be in Luo. Fadumah nodded. Perpetua sang, arms and hips gently swaying. It was unexpected and fitting.

Fadumah thanked them for coming.

Yasser offered coffee and refreshments in the alcove. They all walked down the hall, the mood calm. A much anticipated event was behind them. They could move on. On the table, thoughtfully arranged, were plates of various cold edibles. Fadumah and Perpetua, sitting close to each other, chose fruit. Yasser and Hakim, both having poured a coffee, settled at a slight remove.

Perpetua had expected it would take time for her new volunteer to become useful in the office – and it was taking time – but she liked and respected Fadumah. She had a natural empathy for each individual in the cases they discussed, allowing her to grasp the ethical principles at play. She also paid attention to the specifics of each case, remembering these facts from one day to the next.

Perpetua decided she'd ask Hakim to replace the now spare bed in Fadumah's room with a desk and a lamp, giving her a proper place to work on her language skills in both Arabic and English. Most likely Hakim would ask for assurance he'd receive the same monthly payment for a room with one bed as for a room with two. She'd be happy to confirm it. She had received a bank transfer from Victor sufficient for the first six months, as well as his promise to repeat that payment at least one more time. He had requested – she really should have expected this – a written update on her work. Having nothing new to tell him, and wanting to indicate a certain irritation at his misguided desire for oversight, she simply sent him a very brief thank-you for his valued contribution.

Hakim laughed out loud. Perpetua turned to consider him. She wondered what Yasser had said. She confessed Hakim had charisma. He adapted quickly and easily to the expectations of those nearby. Yasser, about the same age as her son, appeared much more reserved.

She felt the pang of a loved one's absence. He was changing so quickly and, clearly, he wasn't coming to visit any time
soon. She needed to go there, but found the idea of returning to England unpleasant. There had been a time when she
thrilled to live so close to its capital. That was long ago. Now
she saw the country as an emerging security state willfully unaware of the causes of its trajectory. Well … they had their
burdens, which were no longer hers. Except her son remained
there, and had recently accepted a position in the military.

Perpetua looked over at Fadumah. If she wasn't asleep she
was well on her way. Perpetua roused her gently, asking if she
wished to return to her room. Fadumah nodded and stood
uncertainly. Hakim approached, insisting he follow her with
a plate of leftover food. She thanked him with a tired smile.

Perpetua indicated the vacant seat beside her and Yasser
slipped into it. She asked him why Hakim had laughed.

"I was repeating something my brother told me."

"Is it worth sharing?"

"No, not really."

"I have a son your age."

Yasser had nothing to say.

"He lives in London."

"Fortunate man."

"Is that what you think?"

"Why not?"

"Things aren't always what they seem."

"No." Yasser decided he could open up. "My brother was
recently released from prison. I'm happy he's out. He told
me he met a prisoner from Canada who died during interro-
gation. When his heart stopped a military doctor injected a
needle into his chest and brought him back to life. He's still
being held. The guards joke about it. They say even the dead

won't be released; they are resurrected and held forever." Yasser paused. "Maybe it's not funny, but it's why Hakim laughed."

"Did your brother describe the prisoner?"

"He told me he was young but walked doubled-over like an old man."

"Did they speak?"

Yasser saw this was turning into the kind of complication he didn't need. He regretted having said anything.

"Do you know if they spoke to each other?" Perpetua repeated, realizing her interest made Yasser uncomfortable.

"I don't know."

She didn't stop. "Did your brother mention anything else about him?"

"I can't remember."

"How did he know where he was from?"

"I don't know," Yasser replied quietly. "Perhaps they spoke." He looked up with relief at the returning Hakim, who pulled up a chair and sat.

Perpetua considered whether to pursue her questioning. Then, looking to Hakim, she said, "It's possible Yasser's brother has talked to, or at least seen, Mahfouz."

"Who is Mahfouz?" Yasser asked.

Hakim began to point to where the image used to hang, but of course it was no longer there. He remembered when Victor had asked if he could tape it up, how he had reached over the sleeping Yasser to do so. He remembered, too – he didn't know why – two white kittens appearing from nowhere to lap at the puddle beneath the air conditioner, and the moment when he and Victor stood side by side looking over the dark water. Hadn't they discussed the raising of a submerged statue from a city with two names; and how the rising water table leached salt into the once fertile soil?

"A missing person from Montreal," Hakim replied. "Can you call your brother and ask if he would meet with us? It might be helpful."

BEYOND THE FIFTH GATE

Montreal, Alexandria, Crete

2009

CHAPTER EIGHTEEN

THE FIRST USE OF THE WORD now translated as 'freedom' was identified in the legal reforms of the Sumerian king Urukagina. It was composed of the noun *ama*, meaning mother, followed by the marker *gi4,* a present participle indicating 'a return to' or 'the restoration of'. The literal meaning of *amagi4* was 'return to mother' or 'restoration of mother', but through usage it gained a specific legal significance: ending the bondages of slavery and debt, release from the incarceration associated with both.

Aleema considered this meaning at length while walking through her neighbourhood in north Montreal. She admired the grounded quality of a definition both practical and far-reaching. Freedom didn't solve all problems, but restored opportunities to address those that remained. She liked, too, that the concept was based on a desired return to a lifelong relationship with reciprocal responsibilities. She wondered why, in contemporary societies, freedom was always portrayed as a lack of responsibilities, rather than the ability to fulfill them.

After starting her concluding chapter with the Sumerian definition, she outlined the legal reforms associated with Urukagina: the banning of usury; the outlawing of the arbitrary seizure of property or persons; the exemption of widows and orphans from taxes; the assumption of state responsibility for the cost of burial; and the requirement that payments for labour be made in true, not counterfeited, silver. In short, she showed how the earliest concept of freedom was accompanied by a series of laws designed to impede the growth of debt. She wrote that any evaluation of social freedom could begin with three questions: How extensive is individual debt? Are those numbers growing or diminishing? How does debt impact the ability of one generation to fulfill its responsibilities to the next?

To understand the future of freedom within an occupied Iraq, she examined the domestic realities of the occupying power. She noted that the US accounted for roughly five percent of the world's population but one quarter of the world's incarcerated, among whom were large and growing numbers of forced labourers in for-profit jails. Medical expenses and tuition were the primary cause of rapidly increasing rates of personal debt and bankruptcy. Full-time work at legal minimum wage was not enough to support an independent worker, let alone a worker with a family. She concluded that freedom was strictly defined in America as the periodic rituals of public elections to obscure growing debt, incarceration, forced labour, and the policies that sustained them.

The image of an Iraqi holding up a purple finger was not a celebration of achieved freedom, but a selected visual motif to reinforce the new political order, one in which established parties with popular support were banned from running candidates for office, and all government activities were directed and framed by a constitution which the occupiers had rewritten.

In spite of an analysis beginning with Sumer's first recorded legal reforms and ending with the American occupation,

Aleema considered her last chapter incomplete. It was too easily dismissed.

Perhaps Rachel was right. It was the undiminished anger at the core of her arguments that cried out loudest, whether in the lecture or in the book, allowing the carefully gathered facts and calm presentation to be brushed aside as a loser's outrage.

She had struggled to understand the specific reasons for the wanton destruction of her nation, the attempted eradication of its history. A number of justifications existed – most of which had been hidden and denied – yet it was possible to identify individuals and groups who represented those interests and the illegality they condoned. She had wanted to set that information within a context of laws – to force the guilty to accept legal consequences.

That, she now realized, had been an error.

None of the senior organizers of the sanctions, the invasion, the international program of kidnapping and torture – in which Canada, too, had played its dutiful role – had been charged. Most galling was the fact that the extensive CIA collection of videos documenting torture in Iraq and elsewhere had been intentionally destroyed. It was known who destroyed the records, but no charges were brought. To those who ran the country, this was acceptable.

There was, evidently, a shared morality stronger, deeper and more persuasive than the authority of law.

Walking north during her long and frequent rambles, Aleema inevitably came upon the narrow river separating Montreal from Laval. She affectionately called it her Tigris. The choice became left or right. If left, she might go as far as El Markaz Islami or the Madani Mosque. She wouldn't enter, treating them less as beacons of spiritual longing and more as geographical end points.

She felt reassured, however, by their existence and the proximity of the populations supporting them. Heading right, she might go as far as the Greek Orthodox Church of Archangels Michael and Gabriel, located beside the Armenian Community Centre and the Sourp Hagop Church, a mere hundred steps or so from Highway 15.

She stood on that overpass at different times of day and evening, in a variety of seasons, the light and temperature fluctuating wildly, staring at the north-south traffic. The speed and consistency of the streaming currents, each in opposite directions, fascinated her. To jump would make a quick end of it, yet the overwhelming compulsion towards suicide was no longer part of her day. That, at least, was a battle she had won.

When she met Elena, who appeared in the café precisely at four, she had felt as if she recognized her. She saw her struggling with the presence of grief; with the unwanted discipline of enduring it over time. Elena had asked how not to hate those who were indifferent to, or even satisfied by, her pain. She also asked – an amusing moment, if only momentarily – how one could possibly know which way was forward.

They all decided to meet again upon Elena's return from Manitoba. There had been no need to clarify what they'd discuss. Each had a life story so different from the other … and yet …

* * *

Perpetua got straight to the point when Victor answered her call. She confirmed Mahfouz was alive and where he was incarcerated. She had, that morning, met a recently released inmate who talked to him. There was no question it had been Mahfouz. Victor asked Perpetua to hold on. She heard his steps disappearing, then an animated conversation at a distance.

Elena gripped the phone and called out with infectious joy, "Is it true? Is it true?"

Perpetua couldn't help but laugh. She confirmed the good news.

"Oh my god!" Elena cried. "Oh my god!"

Perpetua added softly that while he was not yet released, he had survived the worst.

"Has he been hurt?"

What to do with that question? Broken bones can be reset, memories of the sharpest pain can dull, chronic fears caused by repeated abuse can eventually be put into context and whittled to size. Yet brain damage was irreversible, whether caused by the repeated banging of a prisoner's head against a wall, or the temporary lack of oxygen due to a ligature, partial drowning, or sustained compression on the neck. From the conversation with Yasser's brother it was clear Mahfouz's well-being had been diminished. It wouldn't be the first time a young wife, over-joyed with the promise of reuniting with a partner, suffered heartbreak as she realized he would never again be fully present.

"Interrogations are designed to break people," Perpetua replied. "When you imagine him keep that in mind."

"I understand."

Perpetua doubted that Elena understood, but didn't be-grudge the claim. In a difficult situation everyone wants to maintain the illusion of control, even if it be as slight and ephemeral as understanding.

Elena asked Perpetua to call Mahfouz's parents. She care-fully dictated the number.

"I'll do that right away."

"Thank you."

Perpetua remembered the photo Victor had shown her of Mahfouz, Elena and the young child. "How is your daughter?"

"Sharon is well. She's with Mahfouz's parents in Montreal. She goes to school there. I'll be rejoining them soon. She'll be happy to hear the news. I'll wait until you've had time to tell his parents before I talk to her."

"If anything new happens I'll call you."

"I hope, one day, to be able to thank you in person."

"I would like that," Perpetua said, surprised by her own reply.

Victor returned to the line to ask how she had located Mahfouz. Perpetua kept her answer brief. A new employee at Hakim's hotel, whom she met by chance following the death of Fadumah's mother, had been the connection.

Victor remembered Fadumah's unrestrained anguish while speaking in Perpetua's office. He again felt the enormous stress she carried. And now her mother was dead. "And Fadumah's brothers? Do you know about them?"

"We believe they're in Libya. We're trying to establish contact."

"I understand," Victor replied.

After the call Perpetua moved from her desk to the volunteer's table. She twisted slightly to stare out the window, taking a few minutes to organize her thoughts.

She wondered what actions Mahfouz had been forced to confess. She knew he had confessed something. State-sponsored torture is designed to support false narratives. They travel hand in hand.

Without knowing the evidence against him or the confession he gave, she tried to imagine a path to Mahfouz's release.

There was a possibility.

She would avoid public confrontation with authorities. Instead, she would explore options with bureaucrats who habitually considered themselves overwhelmed. If people in an office convinced themselves they were lightening their load by deporting Mahfouz, that would be an excellent first step. If Canadian bureaucrats felt it would lessen their exposure to administrative blame by letting a court decide his future, that would be a good second step. Prosecutors, if given the choice, might be wary of bringing to trial a young Canadian on the basis of a confession gained through torture in an Egyptian prison. Finally, if it was possible to cast doubt on any crime having been committed – and she believed it highly probable there hadn't been one – the court might choose to waive prosecution and deliver him into the hands of citizens willing to take responsibility for his future.

She returned to the phone on her desk.

She introduced herself, explaining that Elena had given her the number. Ghadir's response was extremely subdued. Perpetua thought Ghadir was preparing for the worst. She quickly told her that Mahfouz was alive and where he was being held.

There was a sustained silence.

Perpetua waited, then heard a barely audible sobbing.

Ghadir gathered herself and with a stronger voice thanked Perpetua. Worried the caller might not grasp the context in which the call was being received, Ghadir added that the line was tapped, the conversation being recorded. Perpetua calmly replied that she was happy to share the good news with whomever was listening. As far as CSIS and the Canadian government were concerned, she hoped they would grasp the opportunity to right their previous wrong.

The intent of the call achieved, neither woman wanted to linger.

Perpetua swivelled to better see the picture of Mahfouz on her wall. His shy but straightforward gaze was now familiar. She liked it. It spoke to her of … hope?

And beside him the picture of her parents.

Her son had never met his grandparents. They passed away while he was a toddler in England. It had been a mistake for her not to have travelled home before their deaths, but at the time she had been indifferent to the opportunity. Her parents hadn't wanted to visit. To them the British state and its military had been implacable enemies, defenders of racist labour laws, ethnic cleansing, concentration camps and systemic torture. Now their grandson had been hired by that military. She knew why. Native to England and with more than a smattering of Luo and Arabic, his superiors undoubtedly saw him as an exemplar of 'The New Britain'. It didn't hurt that he was personable, intelligent, and with developed media skills.

She compared the situation of her son to Mahfouz, then to Hakim, Yasser and Yasser's brother. She might as well add in Fadumah's brothers. Of the seven young men, three were in the military – assuming mercenaries were military – two had found a niche in the tourism industry, one had just been released from prison and one was still being held.

Her son didn't risk being killed or physically wounded – a near certainty for Fadumah's brothers – nor being incarcerated. The field of battle for which he was being groomed was the international coordination of media for the British military. He risked, and Perpetua considered this a great threat, the integrity of his imagination, the only lens through which a better future was visible. He would have to struggle to find it, as she had before him.

* * *

The water reflected the turbulent grey sky. Small whitecaps raced to the shore. Dmitri stopped to listen. He heard the cyclical rhythm of the squawking awnings, the hissing of an animate beach.

"Do you think it will rain?" Aggeliki asked.

"If we're feeling energetic there's a path that goes to the cliffs. If we're hungry or thirsty this is a good place to stop."

"Would you like to stop?"

"Yes."

"Good," she replied.

They sat beneath the awnings. "This is my first time to Sfakis," she said. "The last time I visited Crete was the summer after my marriage. We travelled the north coast and spent a week in Heraklion. Not at all like today. No wind. Lots of sun. We went to Knossos and discussed Minoan civilization."

"Does it interest you, that history?"

"No."

"You are more interested in the present?"

"The near future."

"Yes."

"How is it going, Dmitri, your composition?"

"At the end of the first play there's a call and response between Cassandra and the chorus. It starts as a solo. I begin with the drone of two auloi, leaving a thin tonal space between them for a voice to enter. It forces the drones apart. I mean, I hear it like that. Eventually the auloi return to the centre and fade, the mourning over. That's followed by a melody to counterpoint the dialogue. I want it to remind us of Iphigenia."

"The sacrificed daughter."

"Yes, I want both Cassandra and Iphigenia present in the mind. Do you know *Solveig's Song* by Grieg? The instrumentation and tonalities are wrong for what I'm doing, but it simultaneously evokes a past and a present. I'm trying to do that using a Cretan folksong, or what I think a Cretan folksong might have sounded like three thousand years ago. The first draft is written for kithara and percussion."

"Are you happy with it?"

"It finds beauty in the sadness."

"Do you like Nikos?"

He respected her directness. "Why do you ask?"

"Do you like Oksanna?"

"I find her beautiful and intimidating."

He had created an opportunity she couldn't resist. "And me, how do you find me?"

"You are also beautiful and intimidating."

Aggeliki laughed. "God, you're a liar."

"No, I'm not. I'm really not."

"She is getting very large." Aggeliki, hands in front of her, indicated the approximate size of Oksanna's advancing pregnancy. "When I was leaving yesterday Nikos asked if he could talk to me. Since when does he need my permission? We sat in the kitchen. He told me he knows for a fact that Oksanna's child might be his."

"Might?"

"He also knows for a fact that Oksanna's child might not be his."

"If he doesn't know one way or another why is he telling you now?"

"I asked. He said he doesn't want me to become angry or disillusioned if the child isn't his."

"That makes sense."

"I wouldn't like being surprised."

"Did you ask who the other father might be?"

"I don't want to know."

Dmitri heard a very light but rapid tapping. The two fingers of her right hand suddenly stilled, and she picked up a slower rhythm with her foot.

"What should I do, Dmitri? I don't want to make a mistake."

"What kind of mistake?"

"An irrevocable one."

"What did you tell him?"

"That we'd talk when I returned." The foot stopped. "He's come to life since she's been with us. He's developing policy proposals for a new party. I think they're naive but at least he's trying. He hopes to get nominated to run in the next election. He works on your production and tutors in whatever time he has left. Maybe she'll hurt him in the future, but I think he'll be much stronger by then."

"She wants the child?"

"Oh yes."

"It seems to me the only mistake is acting on a mistake that isn't there."

"That's how you feel?"

"Yes."

Aggeliki felt lighter, unburdened. "I hope they marry."

Dmitri laughed, unforced and pleasant.

"They need to clarify their commitments," she explained.

"Yes. Well … it's not your decision to make."

She considered him. He was easy to talk to and reasonable. She wondered what effect his emotional support would have if she lived with him. She wondered if she'd be able to reciprocate, day after day. She imagined the possibilities of intimacy. Nothing is easy, she thought, especially at the beginning. Nonetheless, they could learn from each other.

"This weekend, Dmitri, this weekend … it doesn't have to be too meaningful."

About the Author

Michael Springate's published works include the novel *The Beautiful West & The Beloved of God* (Guernica Editions, 2014), republished in French translation as *L'engrenage des apparences* (Les éditions Sémaphore, 2019), as well as *Revolt/Compassion* (Guernica Editions, 2019), a collection of six scripts for contemporary performance: *Historical Bliss*, *Dog & Crow*, *The Consolation of Philosophy*, *Freeport Texas*, *Kareena*, and *Küt: Shock & Awe*. He wrote the screenplay for two feature films directed by Carolyn Combs, *Acts of Imagination* (Toronto Film Festival 2006) and *Bella Ciao!* (Whistler Film Festival, 2018).

Printed by Imprimerie Gauvin
Gatineau, Québec